Dear Reader

I have always been fascinated by the lives of pioneers—the men who were brave enough, strong enough, determined enough to take on a harsh, dangerous and alien land and forge a future for themselves and their families. To me such men are a very special breed.

Two years ago I wrote a trilogy about the **Kings of the Outback** from the Kimberly, a family who had become legendary in that vast expanse of Australia. Another part of Australia which tested the grit and endurance of pioneers is the tropical far north of Queensland. Instead of drought, they faced cyclones; instead of desert, almost impenetrable rainforest. Yet the land was cleared for profitable plantations—sugar cane, tea, tropical fruit.

I decided to marry one of the King men from the Kimberly to a remarkable Italian woman, Isabella Valeri, whose father had pioneered the far north. This trilogy is about their three grandsons—Alex, Tony and Matt—and the women they choose to partner them into their future.

These men are a very special breed. Nothing will stop them from winning what they want. I love reading about men like that. I hope you do too.

With love

Emma Darcy

Award-winning Australian author **Emma Darcy** writes compelling, sexy, intensely emotional novels that have gripped the imagination of readers around the globe. She's written an impressive 80 novels for Modern Romance® and sold nearly 60 million books worldwide.

We hope you enjoy Emma Darcy's exciting new trilogy:

KINGS OF AUSTRALIA

The King brothers must marry—
can they claim the brides of their choice?

Alessandro, Antonio and Matteo are three gorgeous brothers and heirs to a plantation empire in the lush tropical north of Australia. Each must find a bride to continue the prestigious family line…but will they marry for duty, passion, or love?

June 2002: **THE ARRANGED MARRIAGE**
July 2002: **THE BRIDAL BARGAIN**
August 2002: **THE HONEYMOON CONTRACT**

Don't miss the **KINGS OF AUSTRALIA**!

THE ARRANGED MARRIAGE

BY

EMMA DARCY

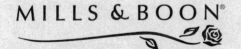

MILLS & BOON®

First published in Great Britain 2002
Harlequin Mills & Boon Limited,
Eton House, 18-24 Paradise Road, Richmond, Surrey TW9 1SR

© Emma Darcy 2002

ISBN 0 263 82936 7

Set in Times Roman 10½ on 12½ pt.
01-0602-41477

Printed and bound in Spain
by Litografía Rosés, S.A., Barcelona

CHAPTER ONE

ISABELLA VALERI KING eyed her niece by marriage, approving the strength she saw in Elizabeth's face. This woman, considered to be the matriarch of the Kings of the Kimberley, understood what family was about—property, heritage, passed from generation to generation.

There had to be marriage.

There had to be children.

Elizabeth had three sons, all of them married this past year and two of them begetting children already. *She* could rest content. Not so Isabella. Of her three grandsons, only Alessandro was planning to marry, and it was not a marriage Isabella favoured.

The woman of his choice was not right for him.

But how to make him see?

How to change his mind?

The wedding date was set in December, after the sugarcane had been harvested. It was May now. Six months Isabella had to somehow show Alessandro that Michelle Banks would never settle happily into his life. She was selfish, that one. Selfish and self-centred. But very clever at wheedling her own way, undoubtedly using sex to seduce Alessandro into indulging her.

How long would that last into their marriage?

And a woman so fussy about preserving her figure…pregnancy would certainly not be attractive to her. Would she agree to have even one child, or would there be excuses, delays, outright refusal?

"This is a wonderful location, Isabella," Elizabeth said admiringly, looking out over Dickinson Inlet to the cane fields on the other side.

They were sitting in the loggia beside the fountain, sharing morning tea, and the open colonnade gave a very different vista to that of the Outback in the Kimberley. Here was the intense green of far north Queensland, and pressing around all the land claimed by man was the tropical rainforest, as primitive on its own unique terms as the vast red heart of Australia.

Isabella remembered how dearly the land had been won; the labour-intensive clearing, the treacherous vines and poisonous plants, the heat, the humidity, the fevers, the deadly snakes. She'd been born amongst the cane fields, to Italian immigrants, seventy-eight years ago.

Apart from the short span of time spent in Brisbane, when she'd met and married Edward King, before he and her brother, Enrico, had gone off to the war in Europe, her home had always been here, on this hill overlooking Port Douglas. This was where she had returned—a war widow—to give birth to the child Edward had given her before he'd gone—their son, her dearly beloved Roberto.

"My father chose the location for my mother who came from Naples," she explained to her visitor. "She wanted to be by the sea."

Elizabeth smiled, appreciating the history. "It's a

very romantic story…your father building this castle for his bride.''

Isabella smiled back at the misnomer. ''His villa,'' she corrected. ''Like the ancient villas of Rome. In the old days this place was known as the Valeri Villa. But because my brother did not return from the war, and I married Edward, my son and my grandsons carried the King name. After my father died, the local people came to call it King's Castle and the name has stuck.''

''Is that a sadness to you?'' Elizabeth asked quietly. ''Having your father's name and what he created passed over for the King name.''

She shook her head. ''My father's bloodline is here. That is what would matter to him. To have what he built remain in the family and be built upon. You understand this, Elizabeth.''

She nodded.

''I am sure you know it is not easy to achieve,'' Isabella continued, needing to talk her problem through with a woman who would comprehend it. ''We have disasters here in the tropics, too. You have drought. We have cyclones. I lost my son to a cyclone. That was a very difficult time…Roberto gone, the plantations flattened…''

A time of loss in every sense.

''I sometimes think it's disasters that forge character,'' Elizabeth mused. ''To rise above them, to endure…''

''To fight. To keep what you have,'' Isabella strongly agreed.

Perhaps it was the vital conviction in her voice that

caused Elizabeth to look at her consideringly. What did she see—this niece by marriage to the Kings of the Kimberley? They were both white-haired, dark-eyed, and sat with straight backs. Isabella was almost two decades older, but she didn't *feel* old. Her face might be more wrinkled and she probably had more aches and pains than the younger woman, but inside, the fire for life was still there, the fire for more to be chalked up in whatever time she had left before death stole her away.

"You have done your father proud, Isabella," came the quiet summing up. "Holding it all together for your grandsons to grow into men and achieve all they have. The tour of the plantations yesterday…both Rafael and I are very impressed."

"But it can so easily come to an end. The cyclone that took Roberto and his wife…" She shook her head and shot a keen look at Elizabeth. "I want my grandsons married with children to safeguard the future, but they are not obliging me."

"Alex…"

"You met his fiancée, Michelle Banks, at dinner last night. What did you think of her?"

A hesitation, then slowly, "Very charming…very polished."

Isabella grimaced at the careful comment, her eyes flashing a sharp mockery. "Like a diamond, all sparkly, with a heart and will that's just as hard. There is no real giving in this young woman."

"You're unhappy with his choice."

"She will not make him a good wife."

An instant understanding. Appreciation, too, of the dilemma Isabella found herself in. Sympathy. And finally advice. "Then you must find him another woman, Isabella, before it's too late."

"I? How do I do that? It is not as though Alessandro would ever accept an arranged marriage. He has the devil's pride."

"My eldest son, Nathan, was frittering away the years with unsuitable women. His real life was bound up in the land, as I suspect is the case with Alex."

"True. And Michelle Banks does not share it. To her it is a source of wealth. Nothing more."

"I went looking for a woman who could answer Nathan's needs. I found her. And as it turned out, Nathan answered her needs, so it is a very happy match."

"You *found* Miranda for Nathan?"

"Yes. And I put them in each other's paths. I prayed it would work and it did."

"Ah! The paths must cross…with perhaps, some clever angling?"

"Nothing too obvious. Some little pushes to put them together. It's impossible to control everything. If there's no chemistry…"

"Ha! What woman wouldn't want Alessandro?"

"The critical point is…he would have to want her, too. Miranda is quite strikingly beautiful. And Michelle is…"

"Ah, yes. A very artful beauty. Skin-deep."

"Sexually attractive," Elizabeth reminded her.

"Skin and bones. He needs a woman with child-bearing hips and a bosom to suckle the babies. A woman who knows what a proper meal is for a man. And I do not mean lettuce leaves.''

Elizabeth laughed. ''Well, don't forget Alex would have to find her physically attractive, too. If Michelle is any guide, don't choose a woman on the plump side.''

''She can surely have the right curves?''

''You know him best, Isabella. I think someone with the right attitude might be more important. A woman who could be a partner in every sense.''

''A partner. Yes. That's what Alessandro needs. A true partner. Who will be happy to have his children.''

Isabella was highly satisfied with this conversation.

It was good that Elizabeth had come to visit with her new man, the Argentinian, Rafael Santiso. A fine man, too. He reminded her of her father...a man of vision.

Alessandro could also be a man of vision...if he just opened his eyes and saw what had to be seen to make everything right. She would make him see. She would find the right woman to show him.

CHAPTER TWO

"Gina! You're wanted out front!"

It was more a command than a call. Gina Terlizzi quickly set aside the greenery she was sorting for the floral arrangements and hurried from the back room to answer it, wondering why her presence was required *out front*. As the owner of the florist shop, her aunt preferred to deal with the customers herself.

The reason was instantly evident and punched her heart with shock—Marco, her two-and-a-half-year-old son, firmly in the grip of an elderly woman. And not just any elderly woman. Recognition of Isabella Valeri King came hard and fast, doubling the shock.

This shop was in Cairns and King's Castle was in Port Douglas, seventy kilometres further north, but the whole Italian community in far North Queensland knew this remarkable woman and held her in the highest respect. A quiver of apprehension ran down Gina's spine at being put on the mat in front of her.

"Are you the *madre* of this boy?" she demanded, her aristocratic bearing taut with disapproval.

Gina tore her gaze from the piercing dark eyes to look down at her son who was gazing up at his captor with something like awe. "Yes," she answered huskily. "What have you done, Marco? Why aren't you in the backyard?"

He gave her his triumphant achievement look, his brown eyes dancing with mischief, an appealing smile flashing from his adorable little face, his mop of dark curls bobbing as he proudly confessed, "I got boxes an' climbed up an' opened the gate."

Which meant he wasn't safely contained here at work anymore. Gina heaved a deeply exasperated sigh. "Then what?"

"I rode my bike."

"He was out on the street, pedalling his tricycle at wild speed, and almost ran into me," came the telling accusation.

Gina stood very straight, facing the music as best she could. "I'm terribly sorry that his lack of control put you at risk, Mrs. King, and I'm grateful you've brought him in to me. I thought he was playing safely in the backyard."

"It seems your son is an enterprising child. Boys will be boys. You must always keep their very active ingenuity in mind."

This softer piece of advice reduced Gina's tension considerably. "I will. Thank you again for returning him to me, Mrs. King."

She was subjected to more scrutiny, as though everything about her was being meticulously catalogued; her long streaky-brown hair, the bangs that swept across her forehead, her thickly lashed amber eyes, her too wide mouth, the bone structure of her face, her long neck, the obvious curves of her full breasts underneath her sleeveless blouse, the neatness of her waist, emphasised by the belt on her skirt, the breadth of her hips, the shape of her bare legs and her feet, which were simply encased in sandals.

It was embarrassing, as though she was being measured for being a careless creature who didn't have enough interest in looking after her son properly. Which wasn't true at all. Gina prided herself on being a good mother. It was just that Marco could be a little devil at times.

"I understand you are a widow."

The knowing statement surprised her into replying, "Yes, I am."

"How long?"

"Two years."

"Perhaps the boy needs a man's hand."

Gina flushed at the implied criticism. "Marco does have uncles."

"You are a very attractive young woman. No one is courting you?"

"No. I…uh…haven't met anyone I…um,…" She floundered hopelessly under the direct beam of those intensely probing eyes.

"You were very attached to your husband?"

"Well, yes…"

"This is not good for the boy—your working in a shop, unable to supervise him properly. You need a husband to support you. The right man would lift this burden from you."

"Yes," she agreed. What else could she do? Arguing with Isabella Valeri King was far too daunting an option. She could only hope her aunt, who was standing silently by, would not take offence. It was a family favour that she had a part-time job here, and allowed to bring Marco with her.

As long as he didn't make a nuisance of himself!

She would definitely be in trouble once Isabella Valeri King departed. However, no immediate exit took place. Despite having delivered her lecture on Gina's situation, the old lady stood her ground and suddenly took an entirely different tack.

"You are also a wedding singer."

"Yes." How did she know these things about her?

"Your agent sent me a tape of your songs. You have a lovely voice."

Finally enlightenment. "Thank you."

"You are aware that weddings are held at King's Castle?"

"Yes, of course." The most exclusive and expensive weddings!

"I am always looking for good singers and I have found it wise to test a voice in the ballroom. The acoustics are different to those in a recording studio."

The fabled ballroom! Gina had never been there but stories about the castle abounded. Was this a chance to be actually hired as a singer for fabulous weddings? Could she ask for a much bigger fee? Travelling money? It was an hour's drive from Cairns to Port Douglas. Her mind zipped through a whole range of exciting possibilities.

"I would require a trial run. Are you free to come on Sunday afternoon?"

"Yes." It wouldn't have mattered if she'd asked for the moon, Gina would have said yes. This was a huge opportunity for her to earn far more than the peanuts she was usually paid for singing.

"Good. Three o'clock. And bring the boy with you." She looked down at Marco whose hand she still held firmly. Amazingly he hadn't tried to wriggle his fingers free of captivity. In fact, he appeared fascinated by this lady who spoke with such authority to his mother. "You will come to visit me with your *madre*, Marco."

"I could have him minded," Gina quickly suggested, anxious not to have her audition disturbed by any mischievous behaviour from her unpredictable son.

That earned a stern glare. "You will not." As though realising her tone was too sharp, she smiled, firstly down at Marco, then at Gina. "He is quite an endearing little boy. I shall enjoy watching him at play. We will have afternoon tea in the loggia and let him run free in the grounds."

"That's…very kind. Thank you."

"Go to your *madre* now, Marco." She released his hand and lightly patted his curls. "And do not ride your bike in the street again. It is not the place to play."

He obediently trotted over to Gina's side and took her hand.

"How old is he?"

"Two and a half."

"He rides very well for his age," came the astonishingly approving comment. "The tricycle is by the door."

"Thank you."

"Three o'clock Sunday," she repeated imperiously.

"We'll be there, Mrs. King. And thank you once again."

Ten minutes to three…Gina slotted her little Honda Swift under one of the bougainvillea and vine-laden pergolas that flanked the steps up to King's Castle. This was the visitors' parking area, and apart from her own car it was empty, which made her feel all the more nervous.

For the umpteenth time she checked that the backing tape for her songs was in her handbag. It might not be needed. She had no idea if she was expected to sing with or without music for this audition. At least she had it if it could be used. The driving mirror reflected that her make-up was still fine, not that she wore much—a touch of eyeliner, mascara, lipstick. Her hair was freshly washed and blow-dried to curve around her shoulders. She hoped she looked like a professional singer.

Marco had fallen asleep in his car seat. She'd dressed him in navy shorts and a T-shirt striped in red, green and navy—navy sandals on his feet. With his dark curls and eyes, such strong colours really suited him and he looked very cute. For herself, she'd chosen a sleeveless lemon shift with a navy band edging the armholes and scooped neckline. Teamed with navy accessories, it was an outfit that always made Gina feel smartly dressed—a much-needed boost for confidence today.

Having unbuckled Marco's safety harness, she gently woke him then lifted him out. Luckily he was never grumpy after a nap. It was like, "Hi, world! What's new?'' and he was all bright-eyed, ready to go and discover it.

"Are we at the castle, Mama?"

"Yes. I'll just lock the car and we'll walk up to it."

"I can't see it."

"You will in a minute."

As they walked up the steps his gaze was trained in entranced wonder at the tessellated tower that dominated the hill. It was said that Frederico Stefano Valeri, Isabella's father, had built it so his wife could watch the boats coming in from the sea and the cane fields burning during the harvesting.

"Can we go up there, Mama?"

"Not today, Marco. But we will see the ballroom. It has huge balls covered with tiny mirrors hanging from the ceiling, and a wooden floor where the boards have been cut into fancy patterns."

The steps were flanked by rows of magnificent palm trees and terraces with lushly displayed tropical flowers and plants and ferns. At the top of the rise, they moved onto a wide flagstoned path with beautifully manicured lawns of buffalo grass on either side. Ahead of them was a colonnaded loggia which prefaced the entrance to the castle. It covered a very spacious area. In the centre of it was a fountain, around which were casual groupings of chairs and tables. At one of these sat three people and Gina's feet almost faltered at the charge of nervous excitement that ran through her as recognition sank in.

Alex King sitting with his grandmother. Alex King and his fiancée, she quickly amended, identifying the woman she'd seen in the photograph accompanying the newspaper article on their engagement. He's taken, she ruefully reminded herself. Besides which, there never had been a chance of her meeting Alex King on any kind of social level—until this very moment. But if ever there was a man to turn her head and make her heart go pitter-pat, he was *it*—The Sugar King.

Of course she had loved Angelo, her husband. Angelo had been real life. This man had always been— and still was—unattainable fantasy. Yet with his gaze directly on her now as she and Marco approached, Gina could feel her pulse racing and little quivers attacking her thighs. He was so handsome. *Manly* handsome. Big and strong and with that intrinsic air of indomitable authority that seemed to say he could handle anything he was faced with. Definitely a king, measured against other men.

He smiled at Marco who had broken into an excited little skip at Gina's side. The smile transformed the hard angles of his face, emitting a warm charm. His eyes twinkled at her son—startling blue eyes, given his sun-tanned olive skin and the thick wavy black hair that declared his Italian heritage. The blue eyes had to have come from his paternal line. Somehow they gave him an even more charismatic presence.

Probably Gina should have headed for the end of the table where Isabella sat. She didn't think. She was automatically drawn to the end Alex King occupied. He pushed his chair back and stood up to greet her, making her overwhelmingly aware of just how big and tall he was. Such a powerfully built man, and her head was barely level with his broad shoulders.

Belatedly, Gina shot her gaze to his grandmother, whose autocratic command had brought her here and who should be given her prime attention. *I've come on business,* Gina fiercely told herself. *Business, business, business...* But it didn't stop her from being overwhelmingly aware of the magnetic maleness of Alex King.

"My grandson, Alessandro," the old lady announced with a benign smile that relieved Gina of any fear that she would be judged as ill-mannered.

She flicked an acknowledging glance up at the heart-stopping blue eyes.

"His fiancée, Michelle Banks," the introductions continued.

Gina nodded and smiled and received a perfunctory little curve of the lips in return from the woman seated on the other side of the table. Full pouty lips, *sexy* lips. It was somewhat demoralising to see just how beautiful Michelle Banks was in the flesh—her golden hair sleeked back to a knot at the back, her face so perfectly sculptured it needed no softening effect, big almond-shaped, grey-green eyes, a classic nose, and a swan like neck emphasising her long, model-thin elegance.

She wore one of her signature tie-dyed scarf tops with a halter neckline—a garment that could only be worn well by very slim and small-breasted women—and the artistic pattern of earth colours was complemented by gold hipster slacks which affirmed there was no excess flesh anywhere on the fashion designer's body.

Gina instantly felt fat. Which was stupid because she really wasn't. She was simply built on a different scale to Michelle Banks. However, that common sense argument did nothing to lift the lead that had descended on her heart. This was the kind of woman Alex King wanted to marry. Would marry.

"Gina Terlizzi and her son, Marco," Isabella finished.

"A pleasure to meet you, Gina. And Marco," came the warm welcome from her grandson, the deep timbre of his voice striking pleasure chords right through Gina's body. "A good family, the Terlizzis. Still in fishing boats?"

"Most of the men are," she answered, amazed that he knew of them.

Many years ago his father, Robert King, had financed the Terlizzi family venture into fishing. His great-grandfather, Frederico Stefano Valeri, had begun the tradition of financing Italian immigrants into businesses when the banks had denied them loans. Everyone knew that the Kings would listen to a deal when more conventional financial institutions would not. Judgement was made more on the capability to succeed than on up-front money, and as far as Gina knew, no one had ever failed to pay back the Kings' faith in them.

"And you're Angelo's widow," Alex King went on, his tone softening with sympathy.

She nodded, even more astonished he knew her husband's name.

"I remember reading about him going to the rescue of a lone sailor whose yacht had broken up on the reef."

"The storm beat him. They both drowned," she choked out.

"A brave man. And a very sad loss to you and your son." The caring in his eyes squeezed her heart. "I trust your family has looked after you?"

"Very well."

"Good! My grandmother tells me you've come to sing for her. You must want a drink first. Please…" He gestured to the empty chairs on the near side of the table, opposite to where his fiancée sat. "What would you like…wine, fruit juice, iced water?"

"Water for me, thank you."

"And you, Marco?"

"Juice, please."

"Only half a glass for him," Gina quickly warned as she settled them both on chairs. Her eyes appealed for understanding. "He tends to spill from a full one."

Another warming smile. "No problem."

"So…you're a professional singer," Michelle Banks drawled, focusing Gina's attention on her.

"I do get quite a few engagements—weddings, birthdays, other functions—but I can't say I make a living from it," Gina answered truthfully. No point in pretending to be something she wasn't. In fact, more often than not she was asked to sing by family or friends with no fee offered at all.

"I presume you have had some training," the woman pressed in a slightly critical tone that niggled Gina. What business was it of hers?

"If you mean singing lessons, yes. And I've competed in many eisteddfods over the years."

"Then why didn't you pursue a career with it?"

"Not every woman puts a career first," Isabella dryly interposed.

Michelle shrugged. "Seems a waste if your voice is good enough."

She raised her perfectly arched eyebrows at Gina who bristled at the implied put-down. Why did Alex King's fiancée feel the need to put her on the spot like this. She was a woman who appeared to have everything other women might envy, including the man whose ring she was wearing.

"It wasn't the kind of life I wanted," she answered simply. "As to whether my voice is good enough, I'm here—" she transferred her gaze to Isabella "—for Mrs. King to judge if it meets her requirements."

"And I'm looking forward to hearing it," the older woman said, smiling encouragement. "Indeed, if it is true to your performance on tape…" She looked directly at her grandson. "…you may very well want Gina to sing at your wedding, Alessandro."

Silence. Stillness. For the first time Gina lost her own self-consciousness enough to realise there were tensions at this table that had nothing to do with her. Or perhaps she had become an unwitting focus for them. Very quietly she picked up her glass of water and drank, grateful to be out of the direct firing line.

Michelle Banks glared at Alex, clearly demanding his support. He stirred himself, addressing his grandmother with an air of pained patience.

"Nonna, we have already discussed this. Michelle wants a harpist, not a singer."

"I heard what Michelle wants, Alessandro," came the coolly dignified reply. "Did I hear what you want?"

"It is the bride's day," he countered with a slight grimace at the contentiousness behind the question.

Isabella regarded his fiancée with an expression of arch curiosity that Gina instantly felt had knives behind it. "Is that what you think, Michelle—that a wedding belongs only to the bride, and the groom must fall in with everything she wishes?"

Michelle gave a smug little smile. "Alex is happy for me to have a harp playing."

"I've never thought a harp—indeed, any musical instrument—can project the warmth and emotion that a human voice can."

"It's purely a question of taste," Michelle argued. "A harp is very elegant."

"Undoubtedly. However, to my mind, even within a showcase of elegance, room could be made for some spotlight on love at your wedding." She turned a smile on Gina. "Are you now refreshed enough to sing?"

"Yes. Thank you." She set her glass down and picked up her handbag. "I did bring a backing tape. Are there facilities for it to be played in the ballroom or…"

"Of course." She nodded to her grandson. "Alessandro will set it up for you and give you a remote control for pausing between songs."

Gina's heart fluttered. Was *he* going to listen, too? She glimpsed a V of annoyance forming between Michelle Banks' brows, but said a quick, "Thank you," to Alex King anyway.

"My pleasure," he said kindly, though she couldn't help wondering if he also was annoyed at this manipulation by his grandmother. It didn't make for a comfortable audience. His fiancée, for one, was bound to be judging very critically.

Isabella stood up—a definitive signal for them all to rise from the table. Gina hastily removed the glass from Marco's hands and set him on his feet.

"Are we going to see the balls of mirrors now, Mama?" he asked.

"Yes, we are."

"Come, Marco. Give me your hand," Isabella commanded. "I will show you everything while your *madre* is preparing to sing for us."

He responded without so much as a hesitation, trotting straight over to her and eagerly taking the offered hand, his eyes sparkling with happy anticipation. What was it that made him so pliable to this old woman when he could be quite obstreperous with other virtual strangers? Gina doubted he would have taken Michelle Banks' hand so readily. But Isabella King…was he instinctively drawn to the power that emanated from her…the power imbued by so many years of being the matriarch of this family?

It was definitely there.

Even Michelle Banks was not about to buck it at this point, although Gina could feel the younger woman's hostility as they moved as a group to the ballroom. It made Gina wonder if Isabella King was using her as a pawn in a battle she was subtly fighting against her future grand-daughter-in-law.

She hoped it wasn't so.

She needed this opportunity to be a straight deal between them, one she could count on to lead to a better situation for her and Marco if her singing was approved. It was a big *if,* given the current tensions that were affecting her. Somehow she had to set them aside, concentrate on her singing.

Apart from everything else, she would hate to fail in front of Alex King, hate to have him feel pity for her, hate to give his fiancée reason to sneer at her performance.

She had to sing well.

Had to.

Or she would die a million humiliating deaths.

CHAPTER THREE

"Do WE *have* to sit through this?" Michelle hissed at him.

Alex frowned at her. "Yes."

She rolled her eyes, adopting the air of a martyr as they followed his grandmother and her protégés to the ballroom.

Alex found himself distinctly irked by Michelle's lack of graciousness, particularly towards Gina Terlizzi. He'd taken an instant liking to the young widow and her little boy. Why couldn't Michelle simply wish Gina well, instead of measuring her singing talent against her own drive and ambition? It was perfectly understandable why a single mother—tragically so—wouldn't want to drag her child around the club circuit.

Michelle's single-mindedness needed to be tempered by an appreciation of where other people were coming from. Apart from anything else, it was a matter of respect for different values, different circumstances. And it wouldn't hurt her to compromise a bit on her wedding plans. Cutting his grandmother out of all the decisions was not good. Weddings were family affairs to Nonna. That was the Italian way.

Given his grandmother's none too subtle comments on the harp just now, Alex realised he should start taking a more active role in the arrangements. There *were* other people to consider besides the bride. He recalled Elizabeth King's recent visit, and her account of how involved she'd been in the planning of her sons' weddings. Nonna would certainly be feeling…left out of his. It was not right.

The ballroom was set up in its usual pattern—round tables seating eight forming a horseshoe that faced the stage and enclosed the highly polished parquet dance floor. They'd no sooner entered it than Michelle parked herself at one of back tables, right next to the exit, her unwillingness to be an interested party to this audition all too obvious.

Doubly annoyed now, Alex accompanied his grandmother to the table of her choice, halfway down the ballroom. He saw her and the little boy seated, then escorted Gina Terlizzi up to the stage to familiarise her with the sound system so she could perform at her best.

Her hand was trembling slightly as she held out the backing tape. Nerves? Distress at being virtually snubbed by his fiancée? The unfairness of that slight, and the realisation of how vulnerable Gina must be feeling, drove Alex to take the tape and enclose the trembling hand in his own, wanting to impart both warmth and strength, wanting to give her back the confidence that had been taken from her.

"Don't take any notice of Michelle," he advised, not caring if he sounded disloyal. "Sing to your son, Marco, imagining you are at his wedding."

Colour whooshed into her cheeks. Had he embarrassed her? Her thick dark lashes lifted and her eyes—he'd thought they were a light brown but close up they

were a fascinating golden amber—seemed to swim up
at him, bathing him in a mixture of relief, gratitude, and
a very touching wonder at his caring.

He had the instant urge to draw her into his arms—
to comfort and protect—and only a swift charge of common sense deflected him from such unwarranted and
totally out-of-place action. The strength of the instinct
both stunned and bemused him. He barely knew this
woman.

"Thank you. You're very kind," she murmured huskily.

She had a wide, generous mouth. All the better to
sing with, he told himself, clamping down on disturb-
ingly wayward thoughts of sensuality and passion. He
was suddenly very conscious of her hand, lying still in
his now, and gave it a quick reassuring squeeze.

"You'll be fine. Just remember my grandmother
would not have called you for an audition if she had
not been very impressed with your voice."

She nodded and he released her hand, swinging away
to insert the tape into the sound system at the side of
the stage. It was unsettling to find himself so aware of
her as a woman. It was fine to give her consideration
as a person, but the stirring of any sexual interest was
out of kilter with his commitment to Michelle. Despite
his disaffection with his fiancée's current attitude, this
shouldn't be happening.

Having switched everything on, he took the remote
control panel to Gina, demonstrated the buttons she
would need to press, adjusted the microphone for her,
keeping his focus on making sure she knew how to

work her performance. Even so, every time he glanced
at her, those expressive amber eyes tugged at him, making him feel more connected to her than he wanted to
be.

He flashed her a last encouraging smile as he left her
on centre stage. The need to put distance between them
had him heading back down the ballroom to Michelle.
Yet he changed his mind halfway, choosing to sit with
his grandmother and Gina's son, rather than placing
himself at the side of negative disinterest. It was an
action that might just jolt Michelle into reassessing her
manner.

The show of support for her protégé earned an approving nod from his grandmother. Feeling slightly
guilty, Alex beckoned Michelle to join them, but she
waved a curt little dismissal and struck a languid pose
on her chair, transmitting a boredom that was not about
to be shifted. Alex gritted his teeth. Be damned if he
was going to shift, either!

"We are ready if you are," his grandmother announced.

Alex concentrated objective attention on the woman
who now commanded the stage. She was younger than
Michelle, probably mid-twenties. The rather modest
lemon shift she wore skimmed a very curvaceous figure.
Her overall appearance was pleasingly feminine, though
not spectacular. She would never draw all eyes as
Michelle did on entering a room, yet Alex couldn't help
thinking a man would feel very comfortable having
Gina Terlizzi on his arm.

The music started. Alex noted her gaze was not

trained on his grandmother, but on her son who was seated on the chair next to the dance floor. He smiled to himself realising she was taking his advice, getting keyed up to direct her song to the little boy whose uncritical love would undoubtedly be beamed back at his mother.

Her voice poured through the microphone, a surprisingly rich, full-bodied voice that filled the ballroom with glorious sound, nothing wispy or weak either in tone or pitch. He recognised the song as a Celine Dion favourite, ''Because You Loved Me,'' and Gina Terlizzi gave it every bit as much emotional expression—if not more—than the original artist.

A touch on his arm directed his attention to the boy who'd been seated next to his grandmother. He'd slid off his chair and moved onto the dance floor, his feet rocking to the beat of the song, shoulders swaying, arms waving in rhythm, his face raptly lifted to his mother who smiled at him in the pauses of the song. He was copying her gestures, her swaying, the two of them joined in harmony with each other.

When the song ended, he clapped delightedly and called out, ''More, Mama!''

Alex couldn't help sharing a smile with his grandmother who was clearly affected by the little scene, her face softened with the pleasure that old people invariably found in the artless joy of little children.

''Yes, we must hear more,'' she called out supportively.

Gina nodded, took a deep breath and started the tape again.

It was certainly no hardship listening to her. As she sang what Alex considered a great rendition of Frank Sinatra's old song, "All The Way," he looked back at Michelle, expecting her to be enjoying it as much as he was. She returned a petulant glare that really riled him. Couldn't she concede Gina Terlizzi was worth listening to?

He looked at the little boy, happily jigging along with the song, and when he clapped at the end of it, Alex couldn't resist joining in the applause. Why not? It was deserved. And he felt a need to make up for Michelle's stubborn stand-off.

"Another one, please," his grandmother requested.

Alex knew most of the popular wedding songs from hearing his grandmother playing them over and over to sort out her recommendations to the couples who booked their weddings here. She'd started the business years ago, determined on maintaining the castle with the profits made—a totally unnecessary decision since the King investments could easily carry any cost to keeping this prime property as it should be kept.

Alex suspected she simply enjoyed planning big occasions and seeing the ballroom put to good use. It also gave her a convenient lead-in to asking her three grandsons when she could expect a wedding from them. She had one now and as Alex listened to Gina Terlizzi sing "From This Moment On," he silently vowed to ensure that his grandmother would have some voice in the planning of it. Michelle could like it or lump it.

Respect was called for.

Respect would be given.

From this moment on…

CHAPTER FOUR

THEY were sitting at the table by the fountain again. A sumptuous afternoon tea had been served. Marco was happily running around the lawn, exploring various parts of the gardens. It would have been the perfect wind-down from her audition, but for the somewhat sour presence of Michelle Banks.

Even so, Gina's inner excitement could not be dampened. Isabella Valeri King had more than approved her singing. She had complimented her on it with open pleasure. So had Alex King. And best of all, she now had Isabella's assurance of a high recommendation for bookings. In future, she would be singing at the castle many times, for a much bigger fee than she had ever been offered before.

It didn't matter that Michelle Banks had more or less removed herself from making even a friendly comment. Perhaps she had wanted Alex to herself this afternoon and resented his being dragged into helping with Isabella's business. Although Alex hadn't seemed to mind the claim on his time.

He'd been so kind and helpful. If he wasn't *taken*, Gina had the funny feeling she'd be head over heels in love with him. When he'd held her hand, and she'd looked into his eyes, there'd been a heart-thumping connection that had energised her whole body.

But she mustn't dwell on that.

He was taken.

It was probably his nature to be kind to everyone. It didn't mean that he was attracted to her, anywhere near as strongly as she was attracted to him. How could he be? She wasn't in the same class as his fiancée.

The home-baked carrot cake with the delicious soft cream-cheese topping kept tempting her. She'd already had one piece. Would it look greedy if she took another? She was always hungry after a performance. It took so much energy. Apart from which, her stomach had been churning with nerves beforehand, making it impossible to eat a proper lunch.

Alex reached out and helped himself to a second slice. Catching her watching his action, he grinned, his blue eyes twinkling a teasing awareness of her own temptation. "It's my favourite cake. Can't resist."

"It sure is the best," she agreed on a pleasurable sigh.

"Like some more?"

He was already moving a serving towards her plate and Gina couldn't resist, either. "Yes, please."

"It's terribly rich," Michelle remarked critically.

"An indulgence in rich food now and then is one of the pleasures of life," Isabella declared.

"If you want to pay the price," Michelle mocked, her gaze flicking over Gina's well-rounded arms.

"Oh, some people burn off the calories easily enough," Alex drawled, then smiled at Gina. "I imagine keeping up with a highly active little boy like Marco gives you plenty of exercise."

Her heart fluttered at the support he was giving her against his fiancée's opinion. She wasn't *fat* in his eyes. He liked her. He had to like her to be defending her weakness for the calorie-laden cake. Or maybe he didn't care if she put on weight. Why would he? She wasn't the woman he was going to marry.

"Marco does keep me busy," she replied to Alex, then wrenched her gaze away from him, bypassing the fashionably thin woman he *loved,* to excuse her appetite for rich food to Isabella. "It's Sunday. I've always considered it a day to relax a bit on rules and simply enjoy."

"That is the Italian tradition," the old lady approved. "Besides, I like my cooking to be appreciated."

"It really is a superb cake," Gina instantly responded.

"Thank you, my dear."

Gina wasn't into the game-playing of scoring off people, but she couldn't help taking considerable satisfaction in Isabella's benevolent approval. Strict dieting could be taken too far. When people took the trouble to provide special treats, unless there was some medical problem forbidding any indulgence, it seemed impolite not to partake of anything. It was like ignoring the efforts to please. Possibly Michelle felt no need to please in return. She had only taken black tea with a slice of lemon, disdaining all the food offered.

Not that it was any of her business how these relationships worked, Gina told herself, but she had the strong feeling Isabella wasn't overly fond of her grandson's choice. Neither was she. Although it could be jeal-

ousy prompting the dislike that was growing in leaps
and bounds.

Marco provided a fortuitous distraction, pelting
across the lawn with his hands cupped together to contain something. ''Look what I found, Mama!'' he
crowed excitedly.

''Come and show me, Marco,'' Isabella called, turning in her chair to beckon him to her.

Her encouraging smile—or her natural air of authority—drew him to the other side of the table and he came
to a triumphant halt between Isabella and Michelle. His
eyes danced delightedly at the older woman and Gina
knew he was basking in her indulgent interest, wanting
to show off to her.

''It's a surp'ise!'' he told her, beaming sheer mischief.

''I like surprises,'' Isabella assured him.

''Look!'' he cried, uncupping his hands like a master
magician.

A small cane toad instantly leapt from his uncovered
palm, straight onto Michelle Banks' lap.

She jumped up from her chair, shrieking with horror,
her hands moving in frantic, scissor-like slaps to get the
creature off her. Perversely it hopped onto her arm before escaping to freedom, and Michelle shuddered all
over at having suffered its touch on her skin.

''You filthy child!'' she flung at Marco. ''Bringing
that slimy thing up here and letting it jump on me!''

She stepped towards him, her face screwed into ven-
omous fury, her long lean body bending forward, arm
outswinging.

The realisation that she was going to hit Marco had Gina leaping to her feet. But she was too far away to stop it, too shocked to even call out "No!"

It was Alex, surging from his chair, who caught Michelle's arm, halting it in midair, his fingers closing around it with warning force and lowering it her side. Virtually in the same instant, Isabella acted, reaching out and scooping Marco back from the line of fire.

"There is no harm done, Michelle," Alex stated, his voice hard with command, the power of the man literally shimmering from him in such strong waves, Gina instinctively held her breath, her heart thumping wildly against the constriction in her chest.

He was defending her son…saving him from the physical abuse his fiancée would still deliver, given half a chance.

"No harm!" Michelle screeched, her body snapping upright, her gaze slicing daggers at Alex for intervening. Frustrated in one act of violence, she bared her teeth at Marco who shrank back, not understanding his offence. "You've ruined my trousers with your filthy carelessness," she accused, her rage unabated.

"Hardly ruined," Alex bit out, his jaw tightening at this further outburst.

"Boys will be boys." Isabella's tone was deliberately temperate but she flashed a quelling look at Michelle as she put her arm around Marco in a comforting hug. "All living creatures are fascinating to them at this age."

"*Cane toads!*" Michelle raved on, her revulsion still volatile. "Ugly, creepy cane toads!"

Marco was cowering back in the protective circle of Isabella's arm, fright stamped on his face as he stared, goggle-eyed at his attacker.

Gina shook herself out of the gut-knotting tension. Her son needed her help, her reassurance. Alex and Isabella King were protecting him but she was his mother.

"I'm sorry the toad accidentally leapt on you, Michelle," she said quietly, "but please don't blame my son for it. Marco thinks catching toads is good. He sometimes helps one of his uncles do it and he's used to being praised for bringing them to him."

Blazing outrage was swung directly on her. "You let him help his uncle catch these disgusting things?"

Gina nodded, keeping her composure very calm for her son's sake. "To Marco, it's a great game. His uncle organises toad races for tourists. He gives them names like Fat Freddo, Forest Lump, Prince Charming..."

"Prince Charming?" Alex cocked an eyebrow at her, his tone amused, although there was no amusement in his eyes, more a wry appreciation of the distraction she was offering. Anger at the ugly scene simmered behind it.

Gina forced a smile at him, grateful for his help in easing the tension and the shock for Marco. "What's more..." she went on, determined on giving her son more recovery time, "...if Prince Charming wins the race and it's been bought to win by a woman, he tries to chat the woman into kissing it."

"Kiss a toad?" Michelle gagged at the thought.

"It causes great hilarity amongst the spectators. They

enjoy the mad fun of it. No one has to go through with the kissing but some do, getting their friends or family to video it so the story will be believed when they go home,'' Gina patiently explained.

"I'll bet it makes a great story,'' Alex chimed in, sealing her account with pointed approval, then turning to deal more directly with his fiancée. "It's all a matter of perspective, Michelle.''

"Ugh!'' was her jeering response. "If you don't mind…'' She tore her wrist out of his hold. "…I'm going to wash the slime off my arm.''

She swung on her heel and with a haughty disdain of every effort to rescue the situation, marched off to the closest rest room. Her snubbing departure left a silence loaded with spine-crawling embarrassment. Gina glanced quickly at Marco who looked as if he was still teetering on the point of bursting into tears, despite the soothing-down process.

Alex moved to crouch in front of him. "Hey, Marco! How about we go look in the fish pond,'' he suggested cheerfully.

"Fish?'' her little son repeated on a slight wobble.

"Yep. Big red ones, gold ones, spotted ones. Let's count them and see how many there are.'' He plucked Marco out of his grandmother's protective hold, swung him up in the air and perched him on his chest so they were face-to-face. "Can you count?'' he asked, waggling his eyebrows as though in doubt.

"Yes.'' Marco nodded gravely as he counted, "One, two, four, ten…''

"Good! Then off we go to the fish pond. If your mother permits?"

They both turned to Gina. She was momentarily transfixed by the burning need to make reparation being transmitted by Alex King's vivid blue eyes. The intensity of feeling bored straight into her heart, forging an even stronger connection between them.

"Mama?"

The hopeful appeal from Marco forced her attention to him. The threat of tears had been effectively wiped out with the exciting flush of further achievement to be pursued.

"Yes, you may go," she said, submitting to the need of the man and the moment, though she wasn't at all sure this was the best action to take.

She watched Alex King carry her son away on a new adventure, grateful for his initiative in one sense, yet feeling hopelessly ambivalent about where this was leading. She *wanted* to believe...all sorts of wild things...yet surely the better solution would have been for her and Marco to leave, allowing these people to sort out their differences in private. Being the meat in their sandwich was not a happy place.

"Alessandro has a fine affinity with children," Isabella assured her, intent on dispelling any worries she might have. "He looked after his younger brothers well when they were little boys."

Realising she was still standing, Gina dropped back onto her chair to show she accepted Isabella's assurance that Marco was safe with Alex. That wasn't the problem.

''He's very kind,'' she replied, pasting a smile over her inner turbulence.

Michelle's rage had been defused but the memory of it was not about to miraculously lift. She hoped Alex would bring Marco back soon enough for them to leave before his fiancée returned.

Though how he could marry a woman like that was beyond her comprehension. Especially if he wanted children. Admittedly, Marco wasn't Michelle's own child, but such a blaze of temper over a little toad, and the urge to hit...

It was wrong.

Terribly wrong.

And everything Alex King had stirred in her this afternoon made his connection to *that woman* feel more wrong.

The fat was in the fire and definitely sizzling, Isabella thought with deep satisfaction.

She had struck gold with Gina Terlizzi and her delightful little son. No doubt about *her* feelings for Alessandro and the attraction was definitely mutual. Best of all, Michelle had shown her true colours this afternoon. In fact, the manner in which both young women had conducted themselves provided such a striking contrast, her grandson would have to be deaf, dumb and blind not to appreciate the differences.

He was most certainly feeling considerable discontent with Michelle.

And it wasn't just *kindness* towards Gina.

But what had been achieved this afternoon could all

slide away if Gina wasn't thrust right under Alessandro's nose again and again in relatively quick succession. The big hump was the diamond ring on Michelle's engagement finger. Alessandro didn't give a commitment lightly. Nor would he lightly withdraw one. It had to be broken.

Determined to strike while the iron was hot, Isabella quickly formulated a plan which she could surely manipulate to serve her purpose. "To return to business..." She let the words linger for a few moments to give Gina time to get her mind on track. "...are you free next Saturday night?"

Surprise at the early date, but eagerness to clutch at it, too. "Yes, I am, Mrs. King."

"I've been thinking...a friend of my grandson, Antonio, is holding his wedding here next Saturday. I would like to do something special for him. It has been arranged for Peter Owen to play and sing. You know him?"

"Not exactly *know*. But I have seen him perform. He's quite brilliant on the piano and a very professional crooner. He really sells his songs."

"Yes. He's very popular. But it would, I think, offer a very interesting variety if you sang a few duets with him."

"Duets?"

"You must know 'All I Ask of You' from *Phantom of the Opera*."

"Yes..."

"I'm sure the two of you could do that song justice. Peter could also do the backing and harmony for your

'Because You Loved Me.' And 'From This Moment On' can also be sung as a duet.''

"But…" Gina frowned uncertainly "…would he want to share his spotlight with me?"

"Peter Owen will do what I ask of him." Whatever the financial persuader was, Isabella would pay it. "You would need to make time to rehearse with him during the week."

"If you're sure he…I mean, compared to him, I'm an amateur, Mrs. King."

"Oh, I don't think he'll find you so." She smiled her confidence. "Leave the arrangements to me. I'll call you after I've contacted Peter. Are we agreed?"

"Yes. Thank you."

She looked somewhat dazed but determined to pursue the opportunity. She had grit, this girl. Give her the chance and she'd go the full mile on what she believed in. At the present moment, she thought Alessandro was out of her reach, but put him within reach…

More importantly, put *her* within *his* reach.

Proximity, natural attraction, the continual contrast between what he had and what he could have, temptation…

"Peter Owen always wears white tails for his act. You would need a formal evening dress," Isabella cautioned, hoping Gina's wardrobe extended to something…fetching. A woman with a fine bosom could afford to show some cleavage.

"I do have one I think would be suitable," Gina assured her.

"Good!" Isabella smiled. "All three of my grandsons will be at the wedding. I must confess I like show-ing off my finds to them.''

She flushed, her thick lashes sweeping down to veil a rush of anguished emotion in her eyes, but not before Isabella had glimpsed it.

''I'll do my best to make you proud of me, Mrs. King.''

''I'm sure you will, my dear.''

And not least because Gina now knew Alessandro would be there.

Probably Michelle, too…unfortunately.

Though Isabella was counting on Gina outshining Michelle next Saturday night…in her own very appeal-ing and extremely suitable way.

CHAPTER FIVE

"LADIES and gentlemen..."

The formal call on their attention reduced the buzz of conversation in the ballroom. Heads turned to look at Peter Owen who commanded the stage, along with the white grand piano which was currently adorned with an elaborate candelabra reminiscent of Liberace's style. A deliberate affectation, Alex thought, as were the white tails Peter Owen wore. Still he was certainly a consummate showman, and much liked by the ladies.

"Tonight we have a very special performance for the bride and groom..."–He made an expansive gesture towards the bridal table where Tony, Alex's youngest brother was also seated—best man to the groom. "...courtesy of our wonderful hostess, Isabella King."

His other brother, Matt, was sharing a table with him and the rest of their party further down the ballroom. Matt instantly leaned over and whispered, "So what has Nonna cooked up?"

"I don't know," Alex answered, curious himself as he watched his grandmother give Peter Owen a nod and a smile.

"May I introduce to you..." The singer/pianist stepped back, his arm swinging out to one side of the stage, his head turned in the same direction. "...Gina Terlizzi."

44

"Well, well, your little songbird, Alex," Michelle drawled, causing the hair on the back of his neck to prickle.

They'd had a blazing row last Sunday over Gina Terlizzi and Alex didn't want one provoked tonight. The trouble was, Michelle's arguments had tapped a guilt in him he couldn't deny. He wasn't sure what to do about it, either.

"*Your* songbird?" Matt picked up teasingly.

"Nonna's," he answered with a curt, dismissive gesture.

Gina was coming out on stage, her hand reaching for Peter Owen's. He took it, pulling her to his side, making a cosy pairing that instantly raised Alex's hackles. What was his grandmother thinking of, coupling Gina with a well-known womaniser of highly dubious charm? The man was already twice divorced, and putting a woman as attractive and as vulnerable as Gina Terlizzi in his path could easily bring her grief.

"Gina and I have been rehearsing all week..."

All week!

And she was positively glowing beside him, a big smile lighting her face, the amber eyes very sparkly, her toffee-coloured hair swinging loose around her bare shoulders, her curvy figure shown to stunning advantage in a bronze, body-moulding lace top, sashed at her waist with a piece of the darker bronze filmy fabric that formed a long skirt featuring a rather provocative side ruffle.

"Hmm...very sultry and sexy," Matt murmured.

Alex found himself thinking the same thing and was

extremely discomforted by the bolt of desire that was sizzling through his system. Michelle was sitting right beside him, dressed in a slinky, metallic-red gown that was braless and virtually backless, so blatantly sexy she'd had every male eye at the wedding giving her the once-over. And she was *his!* Why on earth would he suddenly feel even a trace of lust for another woman?

The thought struck him that Michelle's sexiness was artful.

Gina's was...something else...like a celebration of the woman she was. And Peter Owen was basking in it. No...*gloating* in it!

"I warn you, this lovely lady's voice will grab your heart," he announced fatuously. "So sit back and enjoy the beautiful duet from *Phantom of the Opera,* a song that strikes every emotional chord there is between a man and a woman—'All I Ask of You.'"

Alex found himself tensing as the seasoned performer put his arm around Gina to draw her closer to the piano. The man was altogether too smooth with the liberties he took.

"Wonder if he's got her into bed yet," Michelle said snidely.

Alex frowned at her.

She returned a knowing little smile. "Give Peter Owen a week..." Her eyes mocked any other result.

It was what Alex had been thinking himself, though he hoped Gina had more sense than to fall victim to a flattering seduction. The guy was in his late thirties, not much more than average height yet with a lean elegant air, raffish good looks, longish dark hair with enough curl to flop around when he performed with the charismatic energy that captivated audiences. Gossip had it he never went home to a lonely bed. There was always someone willing—wanting—to share it.

He oozed charm from every pore and Gina was getting a liberal dose of it as he positioned her by the piano, handed her the microphone, held her gaze with a stream of smiling banter while reseating himself at the piano, flicking his tails theatrically. A showman, Alex thought savagely, willing Gina not to be taken in by tricks of his trade.

There was a flourish of notes on the piano, then Peter Owen was leaning forward, crooning up at Gina, pouring an all too believable sincerity into the words he sang, maintaining eye contact as he softly pleaded his cause. Alex's teeth clenched. It was an act…only an act, he fiercely told himself.

Gina's voice came in, soaring with a yearning that eclipsed everything else. There was absolute silence in the ballroom, the whole audience captivated by a purity of sound that projected a high charge of emotion. Of course, the act demanded she aim the words at her duet partner. It didn't mean she was *asking* anything of him. They were simply performing together. She couldn't possibly feel these feelings for Peter Owen.

Despite this forceful reasoning, Alex could not relax and simply enjoy the duet for what it was. In fact, it took all the pleasure out of the evening for him. He was even annoyed with his brother afterwards when Matt commented, ''Wow! What a find!''

And Michelle for adding, "Peter did provide the perfect foil for her. They worked extremely well together."

Fortunately the duet was the lead-in to the formal speeches so Alex didn't have to listen to much more on the successful pairing of the singers. He was grateful for the distraction since it took his attention away from the stage, though he found it a struggle to focus his concentration on what was being said.

Tony did himself proud as best man. He'd always had the gift of the gab and he had everyone laughing with droll little stories about the groom and the changes to his life wrought by his beautiful bride.

It gave Alex pause to think about the changes he'd made in his life to fit in with Michelle, spending less time at the plantations and more on financial management in town, taking an interest in how the fashion business worked. Impossible not to since Michelle was so committed to it. And it *was* a different and intriguing slice of life—colourful people, exciting activity around the creative process. He'd been quite dazzled by it, dazzled by Michelle.

The speeches over, Peter Owen announced another duet—"From This Moment On"—which covered the cake-cutting ceremony. This time Alex deliberately kept his gaze away from the stage, smiling at the happy bride and groom and their posing for photographs. The singing finally came to a halt and conversation picked up again.

"Just a few more months, Alex, and we'll be seeing you and Michelle cutting the cake," Matt commented.

Michelle laughed. "I want at least a triple-decker."

I want…

She wanted to wait at least three years before thinking of having children, too. That had come out during their row last week. In fact, Alex wasn't convinced about Michelle wanting a family at all.

He did. He definitely did. A little boy like Marco Terlizzi…

His train of thought was broken by the announcement of yet another special song— ''For the newly wedded couple's first dance together…''

It was the first song he'd heard Gina sing—''Because You Loved Me,'' and his gaze was inexorably drawn to the stage as her voice seemed to reach out to him, just as it had last Sunday afternoon. She wasn't directing the words to her singing partner who was providing the background harmony. She was facing the couple circling the dance floor, pouring the heartfelt words out to them.

Her body moved in a graceful sway, accentuating her lush femininity. The expressive gestures she made had almost a mesmerising come-to-me invitation in them. The shining curtain of her hair glided over her shoulders with a kind of sensual freedom as she tilted her head to deliver the high notes, and Alex found his hands clenching, wanting to feel swathes of it running through his fingers.

It was crazy…this strong attraction that had him questioning everything he'd ever felt with Michelle. One afternoon's short acquaintance…one professional appearance on stage…what did it amount to? How could Gina Terlizzi affect him with such compelling intensity? He didn't want this happening, putting him at odds with decisions he'd made, giving him the disturbing sense of losing control.

The song ended to a round of applause. Peter Owen moved into DJ mode, inviting everyone to join the couple on the floor and switching the sound system on to play the dance tracks he'd chosen. Alex instantly stood up, determined to get himself *on track* by drawing Michelle into his arms for a dance. He needed to feel close to her again, to feel completely engaged by all she was.

It didn't work.

Michelle chose to dance apart from him, creating a spotlight on herself, much appreciated by the men looking on. She was *his,* Alex told himself, so it shouldn't matter, didn't matter. Let other men envy him. Let Michelle enjoy being the focus of lustful attention. Hadn't Gina Terlizzi drawn the same attention up on stage just now?

Before he realised what he was doing, his gaze was travelling around, searching her out. Gone from the stage. So was Peter Owen. He spotted them both at the table where his grandmother sat, Gina smiling happily at her new employer as Peter chatted, no doubt eliciting praise for their performance.

The strong gut urge to leave Michelle to her admirers and tear Gina Terlizzi away from her slick companion and sweep her onto the dance floor and into his arms threw him completely out of step with the rhythm of the music.

"Alex, get with it!" Michelle protested, continuing to gyrate seductively.

He stopped dead, too unsettled to even try to follow her movements. "I'm not in the mood for this kind of dancing," he stated bluntly.

Her eyes glittered a challenge. "Then I'll get another partner."

"Do that," he said, not rising to the bait, not even caring about it. "I'll go and have a word with my grandmother."

He was asking for trouble. He watched Michelle testily pluck another partner from a group of unattached males and knew with absolute certainty he was courting *big* trouble. But the need to sort himself out with Gina Terlizzi was paramount.

CHAPTER SIX

STRANGE how flat she felt now her performance was over. Gina knew she should be feeling exhilarated at how well it had gone. Peter Owen was delighted with her, suggesting they do more gigs together. Isabella King and the other people at her table had showered her with compliments. Yet she yearned to get away and be by herself.

Stupid to let seeing Alex King leading his fiancée straight onto the dance floor affect her like this. They'd been the first to join the bridal couple there after she'd finished her last song, Michelle shimmying seductively in a slinky red knock-out gown, Alex's attention riveted on her. And why not? she fiercely berated herself. What else could she have expected?

"Peter, bring one of those empty chairs from the next table over for Gina," Isabella directed. "She can sit with me while..."

"No, no, I really must be going now," she quickly protested.

"Going?" Isabella frowned at her. "I intended for you to stay and enjoy the party. Marco is perfectly safe in the nursery quarters with Rosita watching over him."

Isabella had pressed the invitation to stay overnight in the castle and Gina had been tempted into accepting it, not really admitting to herself that the main attraction

52

had been the possibility of some further connection with Alex King. With that barely acknowledged fantasy now revealed as hopelessly askew, she sought a quick escape route.

"The surroundings are strange to him, Mrs. King. Should he wake…"

"If there's any problem…"

The words floated past her, not sinking into her consciousness. She'd caught sight of Alex King carving a path through the crowd on the dance floor, heading straight for her. The couples seemed to roll aside like the Red Sea letting Moses through, reacting to a strength of purpose that willed them away from him. And she was the end destination. His eyes told her so. He didn't so much as glance at anyone else, not even his grandmother.

Gina had the weirdest sense of her whole body being attacked by pins and needles. Her heart seemed to catapult around her chest. Her breath was caught in her throat. She stood absolutely still, waiting for him to reach her, hardly believing this was really happening and nothing was going to stop it. Did he really want to be with her? Did he want…

She didn't dare finish that thought. Her mind was trembling with an anticipation that had shot beyond the real world. But his gaze *was* trained exclusively on her, projecting a need—or a desire—that was triggering all these wild responses, and every aggressive stride he took towards her made them clamour with a compelling intensity, shutting out everything else.

He looked incredibly handsome in his formal dinner

suit. Somehow it made his tall, powerful physique even more imposingly male. She felt her inner muscles quivering and knew she was very much at risk of making a total fool of herself with this man. He struck at everything female in her, igniting a sexual chemistry she had never experienced before, not even with her husband.

As he skirted the table where his grandmother sat, Gina instinctively turned towards him, the people close to her fading into a grey area that held no importance. She wasn't even aware of them anymore. He dominated, his brilliant blue eyes holding her captive to whatever he intended.

"Come with me," he commanded more than asked.

"Yes." The word spilled from her lips, more a submission to his will than any decision on her part.

He reached out and took her hand. Maybe she lifted it in response to his invitation. All she really knew was her hand was captured in his and her feet followed him towards the dance floor. The moment they were clear of the table and chairs, he gathered her into his embrace and they were together, hard muscular thighs pushing hers, the arm around her waist pressing an electric intimacy.

Her free hand rested on his shoulder. She stared at it, fighting the urge to slide it around his neck, to touch...where she shouldn't if any sense of decorum was to be kept. Bad enough to be so aware of his physicality—and hers—with the barrier of clothes between them. To nakedly touch the nape of his neck, his hair...no. It was begging trouble. Bigger trouble than she already had. A struggling strain of common sense insisted a line had to be drawn somewhere.

Michelle was on this dance floor, too.

Michelle could be watching them.

But Alex didn't seem to be caring about what his fiancée might think. Did he hold all his dance partners like this? She was close enough to smell the intriguingly attractive cologne he'd splashed around his jaw—an intoxicating scent that made her head swim with the wish to be even closer to him, to know what it might be like if only she had the freedom to pursue the wild desires he evoked in her.

Could he smell her perfume? Did he like it? His head was bent towards her ear, near enough for his cheek to be brushing against her hair. What was he thinking...feeling? She had the sense of him breathing her in, absorbing all he could, wanting more.

He didn't speak. She was hopelessly tongue-tied. The silence seemed to magnify all the sensations of dancing with him, the rhythmic matching of every movement, the heat of friction making her thighs and breasts tingle with almost unbearable excitement, the possessive pressure of the hand on the pit of her back, denying her any release from him. Not that she wanted to be released. Yet every beat of the music heightened the sheer sexuality of their togetherness and she was not the only one aroused by it.

She felt him stir and harden and secretly revelled in his inability to hide the effect she was having on him, though he did loosen his hold on her, easing slightly away. Not quickly enough though. Reluctantly. Or perhaps that was wishful thinking.

Gina fiercely wanted this evidence of desire to mean more than a simple response to stimulation. It was madness…forbidden pleasure…dangerously seductive…yet she couldn't stop herself from hoping he couldn't help himself, either, that this overwhelming attraction was mutual.

The rather slow track they'd been dancing to came to an end. The music continued almost seamlessly into a much faster number. The couples around them responded to it, but Alex remained still. A sharp stab of panic cramped Gina's heart. Was it over? Would he let her go now? Take her back to his grandmother and return to Michelle?

The turbulent questions forced her to look up, to read whatever the expression on his face revealed. She caught an air of grim decision, his jawline tense, his mouth slightly compressed. Then his eyes were blazing into hers, seemingly demanding answers he didn't have and the need for them was just as intense as hers.

"Let's get some air," he bit out.

He didn't wait for a reply, taking her agreement for granted as he scooped her with him, hugging her to his side while he carved another path from the dance floor. Gina fixed her gaze on the exit he was making for, the exit that would take them out to the loggia. Her heart was skittering nervously. She was letting him sweep her out of the ballroom, away from watching eyes, and she probably should be stopping him but she couldn't bring herself to listen to caution.

The hand clamped on the curve of her waist and hip insisted he wanted to keep her with him. She had to know what this was leading to. There was no turning back from it. If he wasn't worrying about what other people thought, why should she? Maybe he did simply want a breath of cooler air.

Certainly there was a sobering pause, once they had emerged from the ballroom. Had the fever of the moment passed for him? A quick glance at his face showed it turned towards the fountain. He set off again, still apparently intent on getting her away from the crowd of guests and having her to himself.

The few people who had stepped outside remained close to the ballroom. No one had wandered as far as the fountain. Although there was lighting in the grounds, this section of the loggia was in shadow, and Gina was extremely conscious that Alex was seeking privacy. Yet once it was attained, he seemed to hesitate over what to do next. Having come to a halt, he audibly dragged in a deep breath, then gestured jerkily towards a bench seat.

"Best sit down."

He watched her settle on it but made no move to sit beside her. He stood barely a metre away, his tension so palpable Gina found it impossible to relax. Every nerve in her body was in taut waiting for what would come next. She had the eerie sense of being at the edge of something momentous to her life, yet she felt powerless to take any step on her own.

The silence stretched…seconds, minutes…as he brooded on his decisions, his gaze slightly hooded, yet burning a trail over the bare roundness of her shoulders and the slight swell of her breasts above the line of the lace bodice. She could feel herself blushing although the neckline was not daringly low. In fact, a band of the bronze organza under the lace was joined to shoulder straps that stopped any slippage. There was only a hint of cleavage.

"How old are you, Gina?" he gruffly asked.

"Twenty-six." It was a husky whisper. Her mouth was completely dry.

"I'm thirty-four. Thirty-four," he repeated, as though it was some critical indictment of his behaviour with her.

Age had nothing to do with feelings, Gina thought. Yet he shook his head as though the eight-year gap between them mattered in some way. She didn't understand the inner conflict that chased across his face as he moved to put more distance between them, walking to the space between the next two columns of the colonnade and standing in profile to her, staring out at the grounds.

"Tell me about your life."

Again it was a command, yet the need to know was strained through it. What answers he was looking for Gina couldn't even guess. She could only relate the truth and hope it satisfied him.

"I was brought up on a cane farm. My parents still own and run it."

"Where?"

"Near Edmonton, just the other side of Cairns."

"Their name?"

"Salvatori. Frank and Elena."

He nodded. "I know of your father."

"My older brother, John, and his family live on the farm, too. My younger brother, Danny, works in the tourist trade."

"The toad races."

"Yes. Amongst other things."

He turned to look quizzically at her. "No sisters?"

She shook her head. "Just the three of us."

"Where did you go to school?"

"The local primary at Edmonton. Then to St. Joseph's in Cairns."

An ironic curl tilted his mouth. "A convent girl."

Gina held her tongue, unsure how to take that comment.

He continued the inquisition. "Did you hold a job before you married?"

"I worked in a florist shop. I've always loved flowers." Not exactly a high-flying career but it had satisfied her so she wasn't about to apologise for it.

"How old were you when you married Angelo Terlizzi?"

"Twenty-two."

"Very young," he muttered.

"It felt right," she asserted, needing to justify the decision in the face of this far stronger attraction that seemed to just reach out and seize her. She had loved Angelo for many, many reasons. There was no reason at all behind what she was experiencing now with a man she barely knew on any personal level. Yet his compelling tug on her had a vibrant life of its own, impossible to ignore or deny.

She should be asking him questions. But would any more knowledge of him make any difference? Why was he asking these questions of her? Was he trying to reason away an attraction he didn't want, that he found inconvenient? Maybe he was trying to convince himself she was totally unsuitable for him anyway, that Michelle was a much better match.

An angry pride stirred in Gina. She hadn't asked for this. She wasn't *chasing* him. He'd made all the moves, stirring what shouldn't be stirred if he didn't want to explore it further.

"Did you go on working after you were married?" he went on.

"Not in the florist shop. I used to do the lunches for Angelo's deep-sea fishing charters."

And I was more a helpmate to my husband than Michelle Banks will ever be to you, she thought on a wave of fierce resentment over whatever judgements he was making.

"You played hostess to his clients on board?"

"Yes. I enjoyed that, too," she said on a wave of belligerence. "Until I fell pregnant and started getting seasick. Then I did the lunches at home and Angelo served them on board."

Most work was about service to other people, she argued. Even dress designing catered to clients. She didn't see that what she'd done was any more lowly than what his fiancée did. It certainly didn't make as much money but so what? She had nothing to be ashamed of.

"So you've been a stay-at-home mother since you had Marco."

"Not completely."

She didn't want to recall the time of empty nothingness—the shock, the grief, the numbness about any future at all—following on from Angelo's death. Only Marco had been left from the plans they'd made for a big happy family, her wonderful little son who was both a comfort and a reminder of what had been taken away from her. She didn't try to foresee a future anymore, perhaps from a fear of tempting fate.

In a way she'd been drifting, just taking each day as it came, coping more than making opportunities for herself. Isabella King had opened another door for her. Peter Owen might open up more, but suddenly they didn't seem important. Alex King had taken centre stage and she couldn't think of anything else, yet she still had no real idea of where she stood with him. This fever in her blood probably *was* madness.

"You mean your singing engagements," he prompted when her silence went on unbroken by further explanation.

"I'm also working part-time in my aunt's florist shop," she answered slowly, realising the job formed a pleasant stop-gap rather than a step to some reason for being. "I can take Marco there with me," she added, acknowledging what an advantage such a situation was for a single parent who didn't want to surrender the care of her precious child to anyone else, not on any regular basis.

"Who's minding him tonight?"

It burst upon her that she'd completely forgotten what she'd been about to do before he'd taken control of everything. "Rosita. Your grandmother's house-keeper." The reply tripped out as she rose to her feet, agitated by the sense of having selfishly indulged what was beginning to feel like a stupid flight of fantasy, instead of sticking to the reality of a life with her son. "I should go and check on him."

"He's here? At the castle?"

Alex swung on her, his surprise and the sharpness of his tone halting any further movement. Her heart skittered again, setting her pulse leaping haphazardly as the full force of his personality was aimed directly at her. Her mind skittered, too. Did he find something wrong with this arrangement? Wasn't she good enough to be his grandmother's guest?

Instinctively her chin tilted, defying any negative opinion he might hold. "Mrs. King kindly invited us to stay overnight to save disturbing Marco's sleep with travelling."

"So you'll be sleeping here, too."

Tension poured from him, swirling around her like a tightening net, holding her captive. "I've been given the nanny's room in the nursery quarters," she said, then wished she hadn't told him that. Although the arrangement was most suitable for her and Marco's needs, it sounded as though she didn't rate a proper guest room.

This status thing was really bothering her. "Why are you asking me all these questions?" she burst out, her inner anguish demanding some satisfaction. "Why don't you say what's really on your mind?" Her hands jerked out in an emphatic gesture of appeal. "This isn't fair!"

"I know it's not!" he retorted in a darkly savage tone. "I wanted you to help me out of my dilemma but there is no help. I have to make the choice myself."

It fired all the resentments she'd been silently nursing. "Well, how very lucky you are to have a choice. Seems to me I didn't get one. But that's okay. I can walk away."

It was like dragging her body out of a magnetic field to take a step backwards, to force her legs to turn aside from his powerful presence, to will herself into some dignified retreat.

"No!"

He caught her wrist and with a strength that had her stumbling off balance, spun her back towards him. In almost a blur of motion he loomed much closer, releasing his grip to take a far more comprehensive hold, his arms wrapping around her so fast, her hands slammed against his chest in an instinctive warding off action.

"Don't play with me!" she cried, her gaze lifting to his in a torment of protest at his arbitrary use of her.

A dark blue fire blazed down at her. "Does this feel like play?" he demanded harshly. "Did it feel like play on the dance floor?"

Her resistance instantly weakened. There was no stopping his intensity of feeling from flooding through her, re-igniting all the powerful sensations of wanting him, a very immediate primitive wanting that craved action. It wasn't enough to be held in this close contact. It was nothing but a tease, a torment, a prolonging of conflict that begged at least some resolution.

One of his arms clamped her more tightly to him as he lifted the other to touch her face, light fingertips sweeping her hair from her forehead, trailing down to her cheek, feathering the line of her lips, flowing over her chin, her neck, under the long flow of her hair, stroking her nape. The tingling skin-to-skin contact was so mesmerising, Gina couldn't think. The challenge she might have made melted from her mind. Feeling filled it…and the raging desire for more.

His chest heaved against her breasts as he dragged air into his lungs. "I have to do this," he murmured, the low words carrying a deep throb of need that was echoed in the thundering of her heart.

The kiss came hard and fast—an explosion of pent-up passion from both of them, a stampede of tasting, tangling, an urgent assault on any inhibition, a fierce giving and taking that flowed into an all-consuming sense of merging.

Gina was barely aware that her hands had flown up around his neck and were clutching his head to hers. Her body was arched against his, exulting in the imprint of his hard masculinity, straining to indulge the rampant desire to feel all of him. Everything within her yearned to be immersed in total intimacy with this man.

It was as though she had never known what could be…and here it was…the promise of how it would be when the chemistry was perfect, and the recognition of it was singing through her entire body, pulsing from her heart, jamming her brain with a host of needy signals.

Even when he pulled out of the kiss, the promise was still there, gathering a momentum of its own. His cheek rubbed against her hair as he regathered breath, the pressure of his embrace almost crushing as though he couldn't bear to release any other part of her.

''Believe me...this is not play, Gina,'' he rasped. ''But it has to stop now because...you're right. It isn't fair.''

The feverish burst of words floated past her consciousness, tapping on the door of a mind that was too full of more compelling messages to admit them. It was not until he stiffened away from her and the squaring of his shoulders caused her hands to slide from his neck, that the sense of what he'd said began to sink in.

Stop?

Not fair?

He dropped his hold on her, his arms falling to his side as he took a step back, watching her with keen concern as she swayed on her feet. With her hands so abruptly dislodged from his shoulders, all physical support removed, still giddy with sensations that had been given no time to abate, Gina instinctively wrapped her arms around her midriff to hold herself steady. A shivering started, cold attacking heat, the sense of loss growing sharper and sharper.

She stared at him in paralysed disbelief, not understanding how he could *stop* this. Or why he would want to. It felt as though everything inside her was churning around in frantic futile circles, finding only emptiness because the promise of fulfilment had been broken and there were only jagged edges left of it.

She didn't know what he saw in her eyes—the open wound of rejection? A devastated heart? A truth he didn't want to face?

His brows dipped into a pained frown. His mouth moved into a vexed grimace. ''I'm sorry,'' he said.

Sorry...

It was unbearable.

A fierce surge of pride gave her the strength to turn and walk away, blindly at first, the need to flout his belittling apology driving her legs to put a decisive distance between them. The entrance to the castle was straight ahead of her and her focus gradually zeroed in on it.

Marco slid into her frayed mind.

Marco was real.

Her little son loved her unconditionally.

There was a big difference—*huge*—between love and sexual lust.

Best to be with Marco.

CHAPTER SEVEN

MICHELLE felt a rush of elation as Peter Owen tapped the shoulder of her dance partner. "My turn, dear boy," he drawled, one eyebrow wickedly cocked. "I claim old friendship."

She couldn't help laughing. More *intimate* friendship than old. "It's okay, Chris," she assured the guy she'd snapped up. "Thanks for dancing with me."

He grinned back at her. "A pleasure. Any time."

Which was what Alex should be telling her instead of choosing to smooch around the dance floor with *his singer*. Still, darling Peter could make up for that slight. She gave him a simmering look of seductive possibilities as he moved in on her, his long, supple body instantly capturing and projecting the beat of the music. He was definitely the sexiest dancer she'd ever known—both in bed and out of it.

"Deserted by your precious fiancé, sweetie?" he mocked.

"Not quite a duet with your duet singer?" she retorted.

"A promising prospect. But I suspect...more the marrying kind. Want to watch that, darling. Seemed to me Alex was quite hot for her."

"I'm holding the cards, Peter."

He sighed, his eyes running over her salaciously.

"Pity it's the wrong hand. You know I appreciate you more than he does. Do you fancy a quickie in the bushes?"

She laughed. "Too much of a risk."

His eyes twinkled a tempting challenge. "Ah, but the delicious spice of danger…"

"Not worth it, Peter," she said, though her eyes flirted with the promised pleasure of it.

He performed a provocative bump and grind to push the idea further. "He's taken the delectable Gina outside with him. Tit for tat?"

"I doubt they've gone as far as the bushes."

He shoulder-shimmied around her, suggestively murmuring, "Probably headed for a bedroom."

"Alex is far too straitlaced for that."

"How boring for you! Nevertheless, he probably is heading for a bedroom. Gina wanted to check on her son, Marco. Apparently Isabella invited them to stay at the castle overnight."

"Old witch!" Anger surged. "She's trying to make trouble between me and Alex."

Peter exulted in stirring the pot. "No doubt he'll be leaning over the little boy's cot, all choked up by the sweet innocence of a sleeping babe, thinking about how it'll be with his first child…"

"Shut up, Peter!"

He grinned—the devil incarnate. "While we trot the light fantastic, darling."

Grabbing her hand, he led her into an intricate sequence of steps that took them right down the dance floor. He was so light and clever on his feet, it was exhilarating matching him, and Michelle couldn't help thinking how much she missed having this kind of fun. Of course, with Peter, nothing could be taken seriously, but that was his charm. Sheer fun with nothing else attached to it. Free fun.

They stopped at the stage end of the ballroom. Still holding her hand, Peter drew her towards a side exit, whispering in her ear, "Let's snatch a bit of memory lane before the King family noose is around your lovely neck."

It wasn't wise to go with him.

But she did.

Alex knew he should return to the ballroom, if only for the sake of appearances. Michelle would have her nose out of joint at his prolonged absence. He didn't want any sly gossip arising from his exit with Gina. It certainly wasn't fair to have her reputation tainted in any way.

Yet he couldn't bring himself to rejoin the party, couldn't bear the thought of being forced into small talk. It would be easy enough to explain away his actions, but he didn't want to. He was deeply uncomfortable with the thought of skating over what he'd done with Gina. What he'd felt with her...

The restraint he'd imposed upon himself was still a physical pain. Every muscle in his body seemed to be aching, wracked with a tension that hadn't been released. Best choice was to walk it off, he decided. He needed time alone to think anyway.

* * *

"You can't be wearing anything under that dress," Peter remarked slyly, dropping her hand to hang his arm around her waist and feel the unbroken line of fabric curving over her hipline with his usual sensual expertise.

"Stop it," Michelle chided, though she did nothing to halt the wandering hand from sliding down under her buttocks to check the lack of underwear.

It was typical of Peter's outrageous little liberties with women and she secretly enjoyed the sexual kick of feeding his lust for her. Besides, there was no one else in this courtyard. Most people who wanted to smoke or get some fresh air chose to go out to the loggia on the other side of the ballroom.

"Absolutely nothing," Peter declared after his cursory examination. "Which means you're all naked and ready for me."

"Hardly naked."

"Where it counts, sweetie. Where it counts." He led her around a hedge of thickly leafed and flowered hibiscus trees to a garden bench behind it. "Now how spicy is this? You can lean against the back of the bench. The hedge hides us to above our waists. You can watch over my shoulder for anyone coming out of the ballroom while we have a lovely little…"

"You really are incorrigible, Peter." But it was a titillating scenario.

"Mmm…and weddings make me so randy."

"I don't need you for sex. Alex is very good at it," she protested, though she stopped where he had suggested, leaning against the back rest of the wooden bench, her arms casually spread to rest her hands along the top plank. The cooler air—or the excitement of the game—had hardened her nipples and she was very aware of their obvious thrust.

So was Peter who lightly fanned them with his palms as he seductively teased, "Nothing like a bit of stolen infidelity, is there?" He dropped his hands and started gathering up her skirt. "I bet you're all hot and wet for me."

"I don't think I should do this."

"Then you just stand there and chat to me. I'd like that. Quite a challenge operating on two levels." He grinned wickedly as he slid his hand between her bare thighs. "Don't know why you want to get saddled with Alex King. He's a terribly worthy person."

Michelle had to catch her breath before she could speak. "That's the problem with you, Peter. You're terribly unworthy. Can't count on you for any backing if I need it."

"Are we talking money here?" he lilted over the telltale unzipping of his fly.

"Alex has solid wealth. And his family has the kind of prestigious status that adds more class to my standing as a designer. They're assets you can't give me, darling."

"But I *can* give you this…"

Alex didn't know how he made it through the rest of the wedding reception. It was a torturous length of time before the bride and groom finally took their leave. Maintaining a semblance of geniality in the face of

Michelle's high spirits had stretched his self-discipline to the absolute limit. The moment the honeymoon car drove off, he forcefully led his very soon-to-be *ex*-fiancée towards his own car.

"The party isn't over," she protested.

"We're going," he stated curtly.

"What is the matter with you, Alex?" she cried in exasperation. "You haven't been any fun all evening. Are you sick or something?"

"Yes, I am."

"Well, you could have told me."

"I'm telling you now."

She huffed her annoyance at this unsatisfactory end to her *good time.* Alex contained his own inner seething until they were both seated in his Jaguar SL—evidence of his *solid wealth*—and on the road, heading for Michelle's apartment. It wasn't far, just down the road from the marina where her Port Douglas boutique was situated. Rather than be distracted from driving, he did the short trip in silence.

"Since you're feeling sick, I take it you won't be staying with me tonight," Michelle sniped, probably regretting that she hadn't set something up with Peter Owen.

"No, I won't. Nor any other night," he bit out, bringing the car to a halt outside her apartment building.

It drew a sharp look from her. "What's that supposed to mean?"

"It means I'm breaking our engagement. As of now." He switched off the engine and turned his head to look at her with very clear cold eyes. "Our marriage is off, Michelle. We're not really suited to each other."

"And what made you suddenly decide that?" she flared back, incensed by his flat announcement.

"Several things. But I'd have to say your intimate encounter with Peter Owen tonight capped the decision. And hearing how you viewed my assets as a husband."

Her mouth gaped momentarily. Her recovery was fast, though she spoke in a fluster. "That was just silly chat, Alex. Peter is so superficial, it's pointless talking about feelings." Her hand flew across to squeeze his thigh. "You know I love you."

He picked up the all too experienced hand and dropped it back in her lap. "I was taking a walk around the castle. Voices carry on the still night air, Michelle. So do other sounds. I didn't want to create a scene so I left you to it and walked back the way I'd come."

Her chin tilted in defiance as she saw that denial was futile. "Peter and I were lovers before I met you, Alex. There's been nothing between us since and there'll be nothing more. It was just a..."

"Reminder of old times? A fond goodbye?" he shot at her cuttingly.

"It was meaningless," she lashed back.

"Like any bit of infidelity stolen here and there whenever the urge takes you." He shook his head. "That's not the kind of marriage I have in mind, Michelle. Better we go our separate ways."

"Why? So you can hit on Gina Terlizzi without having a guilty conscience?" she jeered.

It wasn't far off the mark and his grim silence lent Michelle the ammunition to fire again.

"Don't be stupid, Alex. Have her if you want to. Get it out of the way."

"And that would neatly excuse your peccadillo, wouldn't it?" he flung back at her, hating her casual dismissal of any honour and integrity.

"Oh, for God's sake! It's like having a brief binge on chocolate. You do it because you're tempted. Once the taste is satisfied, you go off it. You know what diet suits you best and that's what you keep to in the long run. It's all a matter of perspective."

"Thank you for giving me that point of view. It just so happens I don't care to share it," he returned icily, reining in his anger. She was displaying an attitude that absolved him from any concern about her feelings, making it easier for him to walk away.

"At least I'm honest," she went on jabbing at him. "What I did with Peter is over and done with. You're still sizzling for the singer, aren't you? Nothing like frustration to screw up your head, not to mention other parts of your anatomy. I bet that was what you were trying to walk off. And now you're angry because I did what you wanted to."

Her eyes gloated with a derisive certainty in her assumption.

She was wrong.

He would not have used Gina Terlizzi like that.

Never.

He unclipped his seat belt, alighted from the car,

strode around the bonnet and opened the passenger door.

"I'm not getting out until we talk this through," she declared, furious at his action.

"We're finished. I have nothing more to say to you, Michelle," he clipped out, giving her no room to manoeuvre a different situation between them.

She stared up at him in hard-eyed challenge.

No way was he about to budge.

With a doleful sigh she unclipped her seat belt and slithered her way upright beside him, probably trying a reminder of how sexy she could be, given some incentive.

"You'll think better of this, Alex," she purred huskily. "I'm not going to give you your ring back."

"Keep it," he replied carelessly. "Consider it the spoils from the game. But don't think for one minute the game isn't over. It is." He closed the car door to punctuate the point.

"Pride is a poor bedfellow, Alex."

"I can live with it more easily than I can with a string of Peter Owens." He gestured to the apartment building. "Do you want me to see you to your front door?"

She gave him a mocking little smile. "No. I think I'll see you off instead. Who knows? You might change your mind halfway down the road."

It was her choice to reject the courtesy. Alex didn't argue with it. He nodded a cold acknowledgement, said "Goodbye," and returned to the driver's seat, closing Michelle Banks out of his life.

Halfway down the road, he didn't even glance back.
He wasn't consciously driving towards Gina Terlizzi.
She just happened to be in the castle tonight.
He was simply going home.

CHAPTER EIGHT

A CRY from Marco snapped Gina awake. She rolled out of bed in automatic response, then still groggy from the sleep she had finally fallen into, found herself completely disoriented in unfamiliar surroundings. It took several moments to get her bearings. A dim night-light came from a half-open door. It triggered the memory of where she was—the nanny's bedroom in King's Castle—and Marco was in the adjoining nursery.

She started to move towards the connecting door, then stopped, realising it was quiet now. Marco must have cried out in his sleep, then resettled. A bad dream? Since she was up, Gina decided she might as well check on him, make sure he was all right.

A soft murmuring made her hesitate. Was someone else attending to him? Had he been crying for some time before she woke? Rosita's rooms weren't far away. Frowning over the thought of the kindly housekeeper's sleep being disturbed, Gina snatched up the dressing-gown she'd tossed on the end of the bed and thrust her arms into the sleeves. Best for her to sit with Marco for a while, relieving Rosita of any sense of responsibility.

She grimaced over the sensual slide of silk and lace on her bare skin. The coffee-coloured gown and nightie from her honeymoon trousseau were more luxurious than practical garments. She'd put them away...hadn't worn them for years. It had been a silly impulse to pack them for tonight, yet when she'd chosen to, a night spent at King's Castle had seemed special enough to warrant wearing them.

And Alex King had made her feel…well, she'd wanted to feel like a woman again, not just a mother. He'd certainly made her feel it when he'd kissed her. Now she wished he hadn't. It was too disturbing. Better not to have needs aroused when they were never going to be answered. She savagely fastened the tie-belt around her waist, calling herself all sorts of a fool for indulging in fantasies that had nothing to do with real life.

Alex King wasn't for her.

She'd known all along he wasn't for her.

She was a twenty-six-year-old nobody with a child by another man, and he was engaged to be married to a glamorous dress designer who was experienced in leading a high-class, sophisticated life. Dressing herself up in expensive silk and lace didn't change anything.

Having achieved a reasonably modest appearance with her very non-motherly wrap-around, she tried to shove the weight of misery in her mind aside as she moved to the doorway and stepped into the nursery. Expecting to see Rosita, she was stunned to find her son being cradled and softly crooned to by the very man who'd caused her so much heartburn.

She hung on to the doorjamb while the shock subsided. Alex King had his back turned to her but there was no mistaking his identity. His head was turned in half profile, his gaze fixed on the face of the child in his arms. Marco's mop of curls was nestled just above the crook of his elbow and it was obvious her little boy had been calmed and was lying contentedly still, being gently rocked back to sleep.

The scenario her eyes were taking in made no sense at all. Alex King was still in his formal dinner suit. The covers on Marco's bed were flung right back, though she remembered having tucked them in. What had happened? Why was Alex here with her son and not with his fiancée? What time was it?

She spotted a seahorse clock on one of the nursery walls. The hands showed almost half past one. The wedding reception had been due to end at midnight. As far as she could hear, the castle and its grounds were completely quiet. Alex must have taken Michelle home and returned, yet that didn't answer why he was in the nursery. Perhaps he'd heard Marco cry out when he was going upstairs to his quarters, but hadn't she closed the door to the corridor?

It was open now.

Totally perplexed she watched as he slowly lowered Marco back onto the bed, settling him gently on the pillow, then carefully lifting the covers over him, tucking them in at shoulder level. He stood for a moment, visually checking his handiwork, then bent over and pressed a soft kiss on Marco's forehead, apparently satisfied all was well now.

It was such a tender, paternal action, Gina felt her heart turning over. Angelo would have done this if he were still alive. It wasn't fair that Alex King was emitting the same fatherly caring, striking chords that jangled hopelessly in the barren spaces of her widowhood. He made too intimate a connection, too painfully intimate when it could never *mean* anything.

He turned from the bed, a serious, reflective expression on his face, and started towards the door to the corridor. Either he caught sight of Gina out of the corner of his eye or something made him suddenly aware of her presence. An abrupt jerk of his head had him looking directly at her and his forward movement froze.

Her whole body was instantly tremulous. It was lucky she was still hanging on to the doorjamb. It felt as though she was trapped in an earthquake and any chance of escape was irretrievably gone. She shouldn't have lingered—watching him. It had been stupid, dangerous.

Now he was watching her, and even across the room the intensity of his gaze was utterly riveting. It seemed the very air between them was charged with an electricity that had them both locked in a force-field that couldn't be broken.

How long they stood in a transfixed state, Gina had no idea. She noticed his bow tie was hanging loose and the top studs of his dress shirt were undone. He was undoubtedly aware of her bed-tousled hair and the skimpiness of her attire, although the mid-thigh-length gown did cover the more provocative lace edging of her very short nightie.

He took a step towards her, then checked himself, glancing back over his shoulder to assure himself Marco was sleeping peacefully. His gaze swung swiftly back to Gina. She hadn't moved, hadn't thought of moving.

As Marco's mother, it was her right to be here. It was Alex King's presence that begged an explanation.

Apparently he thought so, too. As he stepped closer to her, he whispered, "I'm sorry you were woken. I think he's all right now."

"What was wrong?" she whispered back, maternal concern over-riding the inner turmoil raised by his proximity.

He grimaced apologetically. "When I came in, there was only a lump at the bottom end of the bed. He'd burrowed down under the covers and I was worried about him smothering."

"It's okay. He does that sometimes. Like a little possum snuggling into a safe pouch."

He gestured helpless ignorance. "I thought I'd better check he was breathing and lift him back on the pillow. I didn't mean to startle him into crying out."

She managed an ironic little smile. "Well, you did a good job of soothing him down again."

He returned her smile with a wry twist of his own. "At least, he didn't mind my nursing him. Maybe he remembered me from last week."

It was more than that, Gina thought. Marco instinctively responded to him in some elemental way, just as she did. The pain of their earlier encounter tonight suddenly gripped her heart.

"Why are you here?" she cried, louder than she meant to.

"Ssh..." he warned, once more glancing back at Marco, his brows lowered in concern.

Confused, disturbed, she didn't resist when he proceeded to bundle her back into the nanny's bedroom, following her in and pushing the door to barely a crack ajar, diminishing any sound they made, yet still allowing them to hear a cry from her son. She ended up against the wall beside the door and he was much closer to her, heart-thumpingly close, his hands lightly, hotly curled over her shoulders, burning through the thin silk.

She stared at his throat, frightened to look up at the face she found too attractive, the eyes that might see her quivering vulnerability and the wanton desire for him clawing through it.

"This probably won't make sense to you but I just wanted to look at him," he pleaded in a low voice, gravelled with needs she had no way of understanding.

"What can he mean to you?" she asked, shaking her head in non-comprehension.

His chest heaved as he drew in a long breath. "I was thinking…of how it might be…to have a son."

A curiosity? A yearning? She looked up, compelled to see exactly what he was expressing and he lifted a hand to cup her cheek, holding the tilt of her head while his eyes bored into hers, playing havoc with her own secret yearnings.

"He is a beautiful child…like his mother."

He was wrong. Marco was more like his father. But any thought of correction was swallowed up by the raging need to believe he really did find her beautiful. Her throat was so dry and constricted, she could barely make the protest that her sense of rightness demanded.

"You shouldn't say such things to me."

"Why not? It's the truth."

She forced herself to say, "What about Michelle?"

"Forget Michelle. It's you I want."

You I want...you I want... The words pounded through her heart like a drum roll of anticipation that couldn't be muffled. It was impossible to tear her eyes away from the raw desire in his, impossible to deny her own wanting for him. It surged like a torrent through her bloodstream, screaming for satisfaction this time, needing it with such blind force she couldn't think of anything else. Michelle *was* forgotten. Her mind was driven into a wild chant—*Make it true then. Make it true...*

Maybe his mind picked it up or the same refrain was beating through him, demanding action. His mouth crashed down on hers and a hunger for knowledge of each other erupted—an intense, intimate knowledge that recognised no barriers at all. There was a barrage of deeply passionate kisses, a craving for every possible sensation, an urgency that feared frustration and fought against giving it any chance to break into what was happening.

Action...action...action... The tie-belt of her gown wrenched apart, the silk being slid from her shoulders, sleeves pushed down, off, out of the way...hands skimming her curves, clutching them...kisses, trailing down her throat, over the swell of her breasts, his mouth finding her nipples through the thin fabric of her nightie, drawing hotly on them, unbelievably exciting...helping him get rid of his coat, his shirt, her hands greedily exulting in the ripple of his muscles, his naked shoulders, his back, the dark nest of male hair on his chest.

Touching…with a total abandonment of any inhibition. Touching because she wanted to, needed to, making this intimacy with him so real she was giddy with the intense pleasure of it. More kisses…wonderful intoxicating kisses…her pulses pounding, her heartbeat raging, her mind swimming with the awesome knowledge he was removing his trousers, the rest of his clothes, stripping himself naked, wanting flesh to flesh, wild for the same earthy reality of feeling all he could with her.

And the raw power of this new touch of him had her falling apart, a sweet disintegration that begged for the fulfilment he promised with the hard strength he could bring to her. He lifted off her nightie—a fever of impatience now—his body rubbing against hers, letting her feel, *making* her feel his readiness, *and* her readiness for the ultimate joining. More than readiness. A compelling yearning to give and take all a man and woman could experience together. It was so strong, so immediate, when he swept her off her feet and carried her to the bed, it was like soaring towards a climax and she was spreading her legs for him even as they landed on the mattress.

No waiting. He came into her with all the urgency she felt, and instinctively she locked her legs around him, rocking, rocking hard, harder, needing to capture every sensation, the deepest essence of this blissful merging. Blindly she clawed his back, arched her hips, intensifying the connection, and he more than met her need, increasing the beat of their primitive dance, driving a savage joy through it, injecting an exultation that peaked again and again and again, penetrating every part of her as she came and kept coming until she was sated with the sheer ecstasy of it and he lay limp inside her.

They collapsed together, drained, breathless, slipping into an aftermath of paralysed silence, lying side by side, still touching…but the time of mindless union was over.

Gina felt stunned on many levels. Sexually, she had never experienced anything like this. And it was with Alex King. *Alex King!* Who was stretched out beside her, as naked as she was, and probably equally stunned by this sudden intimate development. Yes, the desire had been there—*mutual* desire—but neither of them had planned this encounter in the middle of the night, nor such an explosive outcome to it.

But it was done now. They couldn't take it back. And in all honesty, given the choice, Gina knew she wouldn't have it any different. If this turned out to be a once-in-a-lifetime experience, then it was certainly worth having. No regrets on that score. So strange— even loving Angelo had not brought this intense all-invasive pleasure, nor such a frenzy of passion.

Alex King…

Alex…

Her mind lingered over his name, silently lilting it as though it had to contain some secret magic. She almost spoke it out loud, wanting to taste the sound of it in her mouth, revelling in it as she had revelled in the taste of him.

Did he have this sense of wonder over how it had been?

Or was he now remembering Michelle?

Forget Michelle!

How fiercely he had spoken those words!

And she had forgotten. In the heat of their coming together, any thought of the other woman had been burned away. What's more, she didn't feel guilty about what had happened. Alex wasn't married to Michelle Banks. Though he was cheating on her, Gina sternly reminded herself.

Was he regretting it? Feeling guilty?

How much did this intimate sharing with her tonight mean to him? Had it just been a surge of lust that was now exhausted? Would he go back to Michelle, having purged the desire that had disrupted his commitment to her?

Gina's heart fluttered anxiously. Lying here in the darkness with him, remembering their tumultuous mating, her body still so vibrantly alive from being aroused to heights she'd never known...it just didn't feel right for it to have no meaning beyond this one night.

"Gina..."

Her name, coming deeply from his throat, sounded like a velvet purr, so soft and sensual it sent tingles all over her skin. His hand slid over hers, interlacing their fingers, gripping possessively. Her pulse instantly leapt with wanton excitement. He could not intend to part from her. Not yet.

"I won't say I'm sorry this time. I'm not sorry at all," he continued, slowly lifting her hand to his mouth and grazing his lips over it as though savouring the femininity of its shape and texture, or paying some homage to what she had given him as a woman. "Tell me you're not sorry either, Gina," he murmured gruffly.

"I'm not sorry, Alex," she answered truthfully, the hope for more from him galloping through her heart.

He sighed, as though venting deep relief. "At least that's all right then. Problem is…I didn't use protection. How does that sit with you?"

It almost blew her mind that she hadn't thought of it herself. There hadn't been any reason for her to be using any means of contraception, so she wasn't. Even nursing a secret desire for Alex King hadn't spurred her to such a practicality because she hadn't really believed anything would come of the attraction. Certainly not this…here…tonight!

Frantically she counted up the days since her last period. Having a regular cycle made it relatively easy to work out her *safe* times. It was over three weeks, which meant she was past the fertile span. Relief whooshed through her.

"It's okay. No risk," she assured him feelingly.

"You're not on the pill," he deduced from her long hesitation.

"No. I never have been. And I wasn't expecting…"

"I wasn't, either." He squeezed her hand, reinforcing the mutuality of their acting without any premeditation. "But I can't say I haven't been thinking of you, wanting to know…" Another sigh. "Earlier tonight…"

"I wanted you, too," she acknowledged quickly, seeing no reason to let him take responsibility for a desire she shared. There was no denying how much she'd craved knowing what it might be like with him.

He lowered her hand, released it, then hitched himself up on his side to look directly at her. She braved meeting his gaze, knowing she couldn't hide from this situation and needing to see what was on his mind. It was too dark to read his expression with any accuracy but his face didn't seem to reflect concern. More a gentle bemusement.

"So here we are," he murmured, as though it were some amazing trick of fate that he hadn't quite come to terms with, although it was certainly to his liking. The burr of pleasure in his voice was unmistakable.

As much as Gina wanted to hug his pleasure to her and blot out everything else, her mind circled his words—*here we are*—and latched onto the big tormenting question... *Where was Michelle?*

Wasn't he thinking of his fiancée at all?

The temptation to keep it that way battled with the urge to ask. Earlier this evening he'd declared kissing her wasn't fair. Had *fairness* now lost all meaning in the face of what they'd felt together?

His gaze travelled slowly over her nakedness and his hand followed the same path, lightly tracing and caressing her soft curves, making her skin tingle again—too seductive a distraction to keep fretting about Michelle Banks.

"You are addictively beautiful...every part of you lushly perfect," he murmured, and although Gina knew it wasn't true, it was so sweet to hear, coming from him, she wasn't about to point out any faults. Besides, the way he touched her *was* making her feel voluptuously beautiful, and it was wonderful to bask in the sense of being absolutely desirable—here and now, when she most wanted to be with this man.

It gave her the courage to explore his magnificent maleness with far more sensual pleasure this time since there was no longer the urgency that had driven both of them earlier. To her mind he really was perfection and she savoured the freedom to touch and exulted in the positive responses that revealed he was still excited by her and every contact she made delighted him.

It wasn't just sex, she thought. They were making love to each other, and her whole being was gradually caught up in a world circumscribed by sheer sensation—the flow and ebb of it, erotic ripples, huge waves of pleasure, exquisite peaks—nothing forbidden nor unwelcome because it was all part of an ever-deepening journey of intimacy that drew them into doing whatever took their fancy long into the night.

No words were spoken. None seemed quite right. It seemed there was a continual flow of communication on a far more elemental, instinctive level…something that words might spoil because they couldn't really express this kind of sharing. Better simply to feel and keep going with the feeling.

It was, for Gina, an entrancing revelation of how it could be with both partners so physically enthralled with each other—a potent mixture of awe and tenderness and passion and sensuality. She was mostly conscious of an amazed joy in the intense pleasure of their sexual harmony, and how incredible it was that it could go on and on. Satiation came slowly, accompanied by a contented languor that soothed them into sleep.

An end or a beginning?

Neither of them even thought of asking that question. Only time would resolve it.

CHAPTER NINE

"MAMA?"

Marco's whisper and his touch on her arm brought Gina instantly awake. She looked straight into big-eyed wonder. Her son's highly expressive gaze flicked beyond her and back again, the unspoken question bringing a sharp clarity to her mind and a shock wave to her heart.

Alex King in bed with her!

She lifted a finger to her lips to keep Marco silent, then quickly whispered, "Go back to your own room and Mama will be there in a minute. Okay?"

He nodded reluctantly, curiosity obviously rife. Gina was intensely grateful he did her bidding without arguing. At this point she had no idea what answers to give him. She needed time to think but there was no time right now. Fast action was required if Marco wasn't to be drawn into a situation that was too complicated to be presented to a little boy who saw things in very simple terms.

Mama had been sleeping with Alex King.

Hopefully Marco hadn't taken in they were both naked. As Gina carefully slid out from under the bedclothes, she was intensely grateful that fact had been mostly hidden from her son. How she was going to explain what he had seen was difficult enough and she

91

certainly didn't want Alex disturbed and contributing anything she hadn't had the chance to monitor first. The situation was highly sensitive, given his engagement to Michelle Banks—was that still on?

She looked back at him as she donned the clothes she'd set out on a chair before going to bed. His thick black hair was mussed, a five o'clock shadow darkened his jaw. Neither factor lessened the impact of his strikingly handsome face. Even with his eyes closed, he could still stir the desire that had engulfed her last night. His wonderfully muscular shoulders, the satin smoothness of the skin stretched over them, the tempting hair on his chest...

She wanted to touch him again, but was he really hers to touch? Was it stolen pleasure? She forced herself to keep on dressing, hands busy pulling on the T-shirt printed with blue butterflies, buttoning the denim skirt, strapping on brown leather sandals. It made her feel like a thief, creeping around the room, collecting her belongings, but she felt too uneasy about the consequences of waking Alex to do anything else.

The need to remove herself and Marco to their own home ground pressed urgently. She didn't want to be involved in *a scene* here. Let Alex sort out his life and come to her if last night held any real meaning to him.

The morning after...

The enormity of what they'd done shivered through her as she slipped out of the nanny's room, closing the door as noiselessly as possible on the intimacy they had shared. Would he pursue a relationship with her or...she shook her head, her mind shying from contemplating any other outcome.

Alex could find out where she lived and worked from his grandmother if he wanted to. A man chased if he was truly drawn to a woman. His arrival or non-arrival on her doorstep would tell her where she stood with him soon enough. Best to concentrate on Marco now.

He was sitting cross-legged on the nursery bed, patiently waiting for her to give him permission to speak, his big brown eyes agog with interest. Gina smiled warm reassurance at him as she crossed the room, setting her overnight bag down close to him and laying the plastic bag containing her evening dress at the foot of the bed.

"Have you been to the bathroom?" she asked softly.

He nodded.

"Let's get you dressed then." She pulled his clean set of clothes from her bag. "Can you manage these while I go to the bathroom?"

"'Course I can. But, Mama…"

"Ssh! Other people in the castle are still asleep, Marco. We'll talk when we go downstairs."

He frowned but started pulling off his pyjamas. Satisfied her instructions would be followed, Gina hurried off to use the ensuite facilities, acutely conscious of the need to achieve a respectable appearance as fast as she could. Although it was early morning, and a Sunday, someone would undoubtedly be astir in the castle and she couldn't depart without leaving a thank-you message for Isabella King. Such kind hospitality demanded courtesy in return.

Nevertheless, she didn't want to be caught up in any long conversation, didn't want to risk any kind of embarrassing situation, not in front of Marco. Bad enough that he'd witnessed what he had. If he blurted out the truth to Isabella King… *Please let it all stay private,* she willed frantically.

It was almost seven o'clock when she led Marco downstairs. Having persuaded him to stand guard over her bags in the huge foyer, she went in search of castle staff and was relieved to find Rosita in the kitchen. The housekeeper's welcoming smile was swiftly replaced by an anxious frown as Gina made her leave-taking speech.

"But you are expected to stay for breakfast. At the very least, breakfast," came the pleading protest.

Gina poured out apologies and excuses and was profuse in her gratitude for the kindness extended to her. Remaining firm about going was difficult in the face of the pressing entreaties to stay, especially as Rosita trailed her back to the foyer, insisting Mrs. King would be most upset not to have Gina's and Marco's company this morning.

"Please tell Mrs. King it's family business. I'm sure she'll understand," was the best exit line Gina could come up with, quickly bustling Marco outside and determinedly heading for her car.

Thankfully they were beyond earshot before Marco's questions started. "Who was the man in your bed, Mama?"

"It was the man we met at the castle before, remember? He showed you the fish in the pond."

"I 'member. The nice man."

"Yes. And the castle is his home."

"Doesn't it have another bed for him?"

"Yes, but last night he came to your room to see if you were all right. He found you snuggled up under the bedclothes and thought he should lift you back on the pillow. It woke you up, remember?"

He shook his head.

"Well, you cried out and I heard you. When I came into your room, there was Alex—the nice man—giving you a cuddle. He put you back to bed and tucked you in. Then he wanted to talk to me so we went into my room. He waited to make sure you went back to sleep all right and we both got tired and fell asleep ourselves."

Marco thought about that for a while, then nodded. "The bed was big enough for him, too."

"Yes." A child's simple logic was wonderful, Gina thought, hoping her explanation would fully satisfy him.

"He *is* a nice man, isn't he, Mama?" came the stress-free conclusion.

"Yes," she heartily agreed.

Too nice for Michelle Banks! But was Alex thinking of ending his commitment to his fiancée? How could he be unfaithful to her and not change his mind about his future course?

Hope moved swiftly into a churning sickness.

Last night had to mean something.

It had to.

Since she could not keep Gina Terlizzi and her son from leaving, Rosita decided she might as well tidy their rooms and take the bed linen to the laundry. Isabella had announced she would not come down to breakfast until eight o'clock. It was always so when she attended an evening wedding reception. There was time to spare.

She entered the nanny's room and came to a shocked halt. The bed was still occupied. By a man! And it looked like…Rosita took a deep breath and tip-toed to a better vantage point for recognition to be unmistakable…Alessandro! A bare-chested Alessandro! And there were his good clothes strewn carelessly around the floor!

It could mean only one thing.

Rosita now had a clear understanding of Gina Terlizzi's early departure. She tip-toed out of the room, not wanting to disturb the sleeping Alessandro. It could be a big embarrassment to do so. Besides, this was Isabella's business and her employer would want to be told at once that her grandson had not spent last night with Michelle Banks.

Over her many years of employment at the castle, Rosita had listened sympathetically to the concerns Isabella had voiced about her family and its future. She was proud of being a trusted confidante and she was very aware that Michelle Banks was not a wife Isabella favoured for her oldest grandson. The plan to put Gina Terlizzi in his way had worked. Although how far it had worked with Gina now gone…

Rosita shook her head worriedly. She wasn't sure it was wise to interfere in other people's love-lives. Strong attachments could stir dangerous passions. But this *was* family business. Isabella would know what to do. She had to be told. At once!

Alex woke slowly, conscious of a deep sense of well-being he didn't want to lose. It was only as he vaguely searched for the reason behind it that the memory of being with Gina filtered into his mind.

Gina…

Hadn't she been nestled against him when he'd fallen asleep? Suddenly aware of being nakedly alone in the bed, he whipped around to check where *she* was, his eyes very sharply open.

Gone. And not one sign of her left in the room anywhere he could see. A glance at his watch showed a few minutes past nine o'clock. No wonder she was gone. Her son would have woken hours ago. And what had felt so very right to both of them in the darkness of the night might not have felt so right to her in the light of the morning. If Marco had found them together…highly probable in the circumstances…how had she explained it?

Alex frowned over that thought. He wished she hadn't excluded him from any responsibility over what had happened. Easier, perhaps. Less awkward. But he *was* responsible. More so than she, since he had come to her. Though not intentionally. After the break-up with Michelle, he'd been brooding over what kind of marriage he did want—a wife who shared his values, children…

Shock hit him. Had he told Gina his engagement was over? What had he said in the heat of the moment? He remembered her protesting his presence in the nursery, more or less asking why he wasn't with Michelle…and he'd replied…

Forget Michelle!

Damn it! That wasn't enough. God only knew what Gina was thinking this morning but it wouldn't be good. His fault. His blind fault for not communicating his situation clearly. He'd lost himself so fast in the seductive promise of all he'd sensed coming from her—all she gave—nothing else had mattered to him.

But it mattered now.

Alex hurled off the bedclothes, galvanised into action by the hope that Gina was still at the castle, lingering over breakfast with his grandmother. It was an outside chance. The doubt instantly arose that she would have stayed on in these circumstances, yet maybe the need to gauge his reaction to what had happened was strong enough to hold her here.

He grabbed his clothes and sprinted to his own quarters, reasonably confident he wouldn't meet or be seen by anyone along the corridor at this hour on a Sunday morning. A quick shower and shave, fresh clothes, and he was downstairs by nine-thirty, his mind having raced through various scenarios and his responses to them, though he could be faced with something entirely unpredictable.

Trying to reduce his inner tension before he reached the breakfast room was difficult. He didn't want his grandmother latching onto the situation between him and Gina before he had resolved it himself, or at least gone some way towards sorting out where they stood with each other this morning.

An upfront announcement that his marriage to Michelle was off seemed the best way to soothe any distress Gina was feeling on that score, as well as distracting his grandmother from the more sensitive area he'd have to negotiate with her guest and protégé. There was Marco to consider, as well. Had the little boy seen him in bed with his mother?

Keyed up to meet and deal with multi-level problems, Alex's mental train was thrown off course again when he reached the breakfast room and found only his grandmother occupying it. He paused in the doorway to regather himself. Luckily her gaze was turned towards the windows at the end of the room. They faced east to give a view of the sunrise over the ocean, if one was up early enough to watch it.

The sun was long risen this morning but the rolling ocean sparkled in its endless movement, almost a hypnotic view if one looked long enough. A coffee cup sat on the table by her hand which was resting idly next to it. Breakfast had obviously been cleared away. His grandmother wouldn't have been expecting him to join her. His usual practice was to stay with Michelle on Saturday nights. If Gina and Marco had been here, they'd eaten and gone before he'd even woken.

Caught in the dilemma of what best to do now, he was still standing in the doorway when his grandmother drew herself out of her private ponderings and looked at her coffee cup. As she reached for the bell to summon Rosita, Alex knew the option of simply absenting himself at this point was gone. Before he could move, her sharp gaze flicked to him.

"Alessandro...this is a surprise," she said with an air of expectation that couldn't be denied.

"Good morning, Nonna," he replied, forcing himself into a casual stroll forward and an even more casual inquiry, "Your guests are gone?"

"If you mean Gina Terlizzi and her son...?" A raised eyebrow because she had not given him that information.

"Gina told me last night you had invited them to stay overnight," he quickly supplied.

"Ah! I did expect them to stay for breakfast but they left early this morning."

Her displeasure was obvious. Guilt knifed through Alex. It was clear now that Gina had fled the castle, fearing major embarrassment. Or worse, humiliation. She had even risked offending his grandmother in her need to escape any unacceptable reaction to their intimacy. He had unwittingly put her in a highly equivocal position and it was up to him to make some amending move.

His grandmother rang the bell and gestured to the chair directly across the table from hers. "Would you like Rosita to bring you some breakfast?"

Odd that she didn't immediately inquire what he was doing here. Needing information, Alex sat down, prepared to chat long enough to find out what he wanted to know. "No breakfast." That would take too much time. "Though I'd welcome a cup of coffee if you're having one."

Rosita promptly appeared and his grandmother ordered coffee for two, not bothering to try pressing any food on him, which was also odd. For some reason she always assumed Michelle never fed him properly and she must be thinking he'd just come from his fiancée's apartment.

"I thought the wedding went off very well last night," his grandmother commented while they waited for the coffee.

"Yes," he agreed. To him it seemed like a lifetime ago—a blur he didn't even want to remember.

"Antonio made a fine speech."

He nodded, belatedly remarking, "He enjoys entertaining an audience."

Tony was an extrovert, always fun company. Alex sometimes wished he had his younger brother's bright *joie de vivre,* his ability to simply let go and move with the flow. *You try to keep control of too much, Alex,* Tony often teased him, but control had gone right out the door last night.

"And my new find—Gina Terlizzi—sang beautifully," his grandmother went on.

"I thought so, too," he muttered, turning his gaze to the view, not wanting his grandmother to see how deeply her protégé affected him.

Her ensuing silence gave him the strong impression that she knew and was waiting for him to comment further. Of course she had seen him sweep Gina into dancing with him and probably watched their exit from the ballroom. Not exactly the action of a disinterested man. But she couldn't know what else had transpired between them.

Certainly he had to inform his grandmother that *his* wedding was now cancelled, releasing the date for a booking by some other couple. There was no possibility of any reconnection with Michelle. Even without the attraction to Gina, no way would he reconsider marriage to a woman who could be so blithely unfaithful.

Which brought him straight back to the impression Gina must have taken away with her—of him having cheated on his fiancée. It was intolerable. Never mind that the desire which had exploded between them last night had been mutual. He'd pushed it and taken what he wanted without clearing the way first.

Rosita returned with freshly percolated coffee and the accompaniments. He turned to smile his thanks but the smile wasn't returned. She seemed to evade looking at him, busily laying everything out on the table. It was not like the usually voluble Rosita to remain silent, and skipping out of the room the moment she was done.

Something was very wrong here. Rosita had been working at the castle since he was a boy and always had a smile for him. Alex directed a quick searching look at his grandmother. Her eyes were half veiled as she poured out the coffee, her facial expression giving nothing away. It struck Alex she appeared too calm, too composed, which was invariably her manner when faced with trouble.

''What's the problem, Nonna?''

She finished pouring, set the coffeepot down, then

met his probing gaze with a very sharp directness. "You are the problem, Alessandro," she stated unequivocally.

He realised instantly that they knew—both Rosita and his grandmother *knew* he'd slept with Gina. Damage control leapt to the fore.

"I'm sorry you are distressed by my actions. I'll redress any problems I've caused very shortly," he promised.

"And just how do you propose to correct the situation?" came the pointed demand, her eyes biting with reproof. "I might remind you…"

"I broke my engagement to Michelle last night," he interjected. "As soon as the wedding was over. The parting was decisive before I came home."

Her eyes flashed some other strong feeling before she sat back with an air of relief. "It is good to know you have not acted entirely dishonourably."

"Nonna, I assure you…"

"Let me put it quite plainly, Alessandro," she interrupted, determination blazing at him. "Gina Terlizzi was my guest. She was entitled to the safe privacy of the suite given to her and her son. I do not believe for one moment that she invited you into it. Her hasty departure early this morning speaks volumes to *me*…if not to *you*."

He frowned. "Did she say anything?"

"Do you expect a young lady of any dignity to blurt out that my grandson had seduced her?"

"There was no seduction," he curtly protested.

"That he used her on the rebound from breaking up with another woman?"

"No!" His fist crashed down on the table as he pushed up from his chair. "Just stay out of this, Nonna! I'll fix it!"

"See that you do, Alessandro," she fiercely retorted. "I do not like to feel ashamed of my grandson."

Ashamed?

It stung him more than anything else she could have said, stung him into a more sober re-appraisal of his conduct, stung him out of the anger that had surged at her accusatory assumptions. His grandmother was trying to see through Gina's eyes, read her reasons for leaving as she had. The reasons weren't right. But it was clear his grandmother's sympathy was very much on Gina Terlizzi's side.

He stood still, understanding the attack on his character, though to his mind it wasn't warranted. "You like her," he said quietly.

"Yes, I do. She has solid worth. It pains me that she should be hurt through any association with my family."

He nodded. *Solid worth.* His grandmother had never really taken to Michelle. He'd excused it on the grounds that she was old, old-fashioned, not in tune with today's world and Michelle was very much the modern woman. As it had turned out, perhaps he was old-fashioned, too. Certainly *solid worth* now had more appeal to him than superficial glamour.

"It wasn't seduction, Nonna. Nor was it a rebound reaction on my part. It was mutual attraction. Which I intend to pursue," he declared, wanting the murky air between them cleared.

His grandmother closed her eyes and breathed a deep sigh of relief. "You'll find Gina Terlizzi's telephone number and address in my office diary."

"Thank you. If you'll excuse me?"

She nodded. "Please take care, Alessandro." Her lids lifted, her eyes delivering an eloquent look of warning. "No one can sing like that without a feeling heart."

"Do you think I don't know it?" he answered with considerable irony. "My judgement may have been astray with Michelle but I'm learning, Nonna. I'm learning."

He left the breakfast room, intent on learning more.

CHAPTER TEN

GINA stood at the kitchen sink, idly washing the breakfast dishes as she watched Marco through the window.
He was wheeling his little trolley around, pausing at
chosen places to set a plastic block on the lawn, creating
a pattern that satisfied his eye for whatever game he had
in mind.

It was a good backyard for him to play in, securely
fenced, with a small vegetable garden adding the interest of watching things grow and picking them when
they were ready to be picked—tomatoes, capsicum, cu-
cumbers. Gina grew the flowers she loved in the front
garden, ensuring they wouldn't be damaged by bounc-
ing balls.

The house itself was an old wooden Queenslander,
built high to catch breezes, verandas providing shade
from the hot sun. It was nothing grand or flash—certainly no castle—but it was a home, a home of their
own which both Angelo's parents and hers had helped
them buy to start off their marriage. Except she no
longer had a husband and Marco didn't have a father.

Was it a wild fantasy that Alex King might fill those
roles?

Last night…caring for Marco…loving her…

She heaved a sigh loaded with all the inner miseries
that had been building up over his connection to

Michelle Banks. Maybe Alex and his fiancée had been at odds with each other at the wedding, ending with a big argument, passions erupting. People could go off the rails at such times, but given a day or two to cool down…

The telephone rang.

Gina lifted her hands out of the soapy water and hurriedly dried them on a tea-towel as she moved to pick up the receiver. It was probably her mother calling, wanting to know how the gig had gone at the castle—such an honour to be asked to sing by Isabella King.

Gina grimaced at the need to sound bright and cheerful, pretending nothing of a disturbing nature had happened…like having taken a lover in the middle of the night and not knowing whether he'd even want to remember it in the morning.

"Hi! Gina here," she announced, forcing a lightness into her voice she didn't feel.

"Gina, it's Alex King," came the strongly spoken reply, instantly spinning her into emotional turmoil.

The shock of hearing from him so soon when she'd been thinking she might not hear from him at all, left her totally speechless. Her gaze darted to the kitchen clock. It was only a few minutes past ten. Had he just woken and found her gone? Was he calling to say it had been a *mistake?*

Her heart seemed to be thundering in her ears. Her chest was so tight, she could barely breathe. Her hand gripped the receiver with knuckle-white intensity. Her mind willed him to say something good, something that would ease this awful tension and give her back the sense of peace and pleasure that had been eaten away by doubts and fears.

"I understand you felt it was the discreet thing to do...leaving early this morning," he went on, his deep voice seeming to throb in time with her pulse. "But can we meet today?"

Meet...today...

For the life of her she couldn't get her tongue around a reply. She was dizzy with shock and joy. It seemed he didn't want to forget that last night had ever been. He wanted to be with her again. But...for what purpose? He might be feeling the need to explain himself, excuse himself...

"Gina...?"

She tried to work some moisture into her mouth. Her heart was screaming *yes* to the meeting, no matter what, but her sense of rightness cried out for more from him. If he was still tied to that woman, why go so far as to ask for a meeting? Did he mean to test his feelings? Or...her stomach cramped...was he hoping to have a fling on the side?

"Gina, I'm no longer committed to the relationship I had with Michelle," he stated in a rush. "I broke my engagement to her after the wedding, when I took her home. There's no barrier to..." He paused, obviously hunting for inoffensive words. "I mean there's no reason for you to be concerned about my playing anyone false. Please believe that."

He was finished with Michelle Banks! This news was like a star burst going off in Gina's head.

"I should have told you so last night," he said regretfully. "And I apologise very sincerely for any grief it's given you this morning."

Her relief whooshed out in a heartfelt sigh. "Thank you, Alex. It did worry me." *Understatement of the year,* but it didn't matter now. The weight of misery had lifted and her blood was zinging with a bubbling fountain of hope.

"I would like very much to spend some time with you today," he pressed. "Could I bring a picnic lunch and take you and Marco out somewhere?"

Such an invitation, including her son, surely meant he anticipated enjoying their company. "I'd like that," she answered, trying not to sound over-the-moon eager. "Crystal Cascades is a lovely place for a picnic, and it's not far from here. I live at Redlynch, on the outskirts of Cairns."

"I know. My grandmother gave me your address."

Another shock, mixed with a surge of pleasure at this proof there was nothing hidden about his intentions. "You spoke to her about me?" The words spilled out, artlessly revealing her need for any relationship between them to be openly acknowledged.

"A little while ago. If I pick you up at twelve o'clock, will that suit?"

"Yes," she answered dazedly, unbelievably happy at this train of events. "We'll be ready."

"Good! I'll see you then."

A picnic with Alex King! Gina hugged the telephone receiver to her heart. It was really happening. Not a completely wild dream. Alex wanted to be with her and Marco!

*   *   *

A picnic! Alex set the receiver down, a triumphant sense of achievement sliding into bemusement over the meeting he'd arranged. When was the last time he'd been on a picnic? He couldn't remember. Yet the idea had popped straight into his mind…Gina, Marco, family picnic. It formed a seductive picture. Which gave him pause for thought.

Was he reacting against Michelle?

Reacting against the pattern of Sunday brunch at some fashionable waterside restaurant…idle chitchat with fashionable acquaintances?

He certainly felt a strong desire to remove himself from that entire scene, to move towards something else. Right now, Gina Terlizzi and her son formed the focus of a new direction, but maybe he should move forward with more caution, more consideration, instead of plunging headlong into another serious involvement.

He'd made a bad mistake with Michelle.

Could he trust his instincts with Gina?

His grandmother's warning came sharply to mind— *Please take care, Alessandro.*

He should.

He would.

Control was the key.

Yet with Gina…did he want to control the feelings she stirred? Was he even able to? All he knew was the need to see her, be with her, know more of her, was compelling, and no way was he about to deny himself this course of action.

*   *   *

Gina was still floating on a cloud of happiness when her mother telephoned a half hour after the call from Alex. There was no need for any pretence to be cheerful. A natural joy lilted through her voice as she answered the flurry of questions about the wedding.

"So the duets were well received," her mother concluded with satisfaction.

"Absolutely," Gina enthused. "Mrs. King was delighted with the double act, and Peter Owen said he'd contact me about doing more with him."

"Well, that is a compliment, coming from a real professional. Not that your voice isn't lovely," she added with a warm ring of pride.

Gina laughed. "I know what you mean, but I don't know how serious he was. Peter Owen is the kind of guy who pours out flattery."

"You must come over for lunch and tell me all about it."

"Mum, I really have no more to tell," Gina quickly protested, though she hadn't mentioned the most important development from last night. A deep residue of fear and doubt seeded a reluctance to speak of Alex King to her mother. Not yet, she argued cautiously. Not until she was sure of what Alex actually wanted from their meeting today. "Actually, I've promised Marco a picnic so I can't come anyway," she excused. "Though thanks for the invite."

"Oh! Well, I'll catch up with you during the week. Give Marco my love. No, put him on the 'phone. I'll have a chat to him myself."

She couldn't risk Marco blurting out about the man

who'd slept with Mama. "He's outside playing. Leave it 'til next time. Okay?" Hopefully he'd forget that highly sensitive information in the excitement of more recent events before he did speak to her mother.

"Of course. I'm so glad you've had this opportunity, Gina. I'll go and tell your father you were a big success."

"Thanks, Mum. Bye for now."

Gina put the receiver down more thoughtfully this time, having reached the sobering realisation that while she certainly *matched* Alex King in bed, he might not see her as his match in other areas of his life. She remembered all the questions he had asked about her family and background after they'd danced, before he'd kissed her and then declared he wasn't being fair.

Not fair to kiss her while he was committed to marry Michelle Banks, or not fair, given her life would never meld with his? Sexual attraction had nothing to do with either. She'd had proof enough of that reality. In the darkness of the night, hadn't their desire for each other overridden every other sensibility? It was true of her, and most probably true of him, too.

Detaching himself from Michelle Banks might not mean anything in the long run, except he'd decided he didn't want to be married to the glamorous designer. It didn't mean he'd prefer Gina as his wife. She had to be very careful not to assume too much from Alex's wish to spend time with her today. The intimacy they had shared last night was fresh in his mind. He could be feeling guilty about it, simply wanting to clear himself with her.

On the other hand, he could have done that with his phone call, so it seemed more likely he did want to pursue the attraction. Besides, there really was no point in stewing over where it would or could lead. Gina knew in her heart, however reckless and wanton it might be, she was not about to deny herself the chance of any kind of relationship with Alex King. As far as she was concerned, it was a once-in-a-lifetime chance.

The plain truth was she didn't want to talk it over with her mother or anyone else, didn't want to hear doubts and fears and cautions. She could think up enough of them herself. Whatever the consequences, she was going to listen to her heart, first and foremost. Surely instincts were more important than opinions shaped by other factors.

Twelve o'clock. Gina had decided not to change the clothes she'd dressed herself and Marco in this morning. A picnic was a picnic, and she liked the outfit she'd planned to wear for breakfast at the castle, though ironically enough, there were more butterflies in her stomach right now than there were on the top that went with her denim skirt.

They turned into a wildly fluttering flock when Marco charged down the hall, yelling, ''He's here, Mama! He's got a big cruiser like Uncle Danny's.''

A four-wheel-drive vehicle, not a flash car. The thought instantly zipped into her mind that he'd undoubtedly driven something else on his dates with Michelle Banks. *Stop it!* she fiercely berated herself. This was a picnic, not a fancy outing. Besides, she couldn't imagine he'd have a child-safety seat for Marco, so they would have to go in her car anyway.

She picked up the all-purpose bag she had prepared to cover all contingencies for her son—Alex could hardly be expected to know a little child's needs or the accidents that could occur—and took a deep breath as she headed for the front door, pulled along by a highly excited Marco who was determinedly leading her out to "the nice man."

They stepped onto the veranda just as Alex started up the steps to it. He paused, looking at them both, as though taking a moment to assess what he was doing here. He was dressed in blue jeans and a royal-blue sports shirt, making the blue of his eyes so vivid, Gina couldn't tear her own gaze away from them. All her insides were helplessly aquiver, waiting for his judgement. Then he smiled and the nervous flutters melted in a wave of warm pleasure.

"Hi! It's good to see you again," he declared, including her son in the greeting. "Remember me, Marco? My name is Alex."

"Yes, I 'member. You weren't scared of the cane toad and you showed me the pretty fish," Marco smugly informed him.

Alex laughed, delighted by the recognition given. "Well, maybe we'll find something exciting to do this afternoon. I'll just carry your mother's bag for her and off we'll go." He acted on his words, remarking ironically, "You didn't need to bring anything, Gina."

"It's just stuff for Marco. I wasn't sure…"

"I figured all little boys like barbecued chicken, bananas and ice blocks.'' His eyes twinkled teasingly. ''Right or wrong?''

She had to smile at his forethought. ''Right enough.'' They were down the steps and following the path to the front gate before she remembered the transport problem. ''You won't have a car seat for him. I thought...''

''Yes, I have. Got one installed at a hire-car place.''

She stopped, amazed at the trouble he'd gone to.

''I did ask you both out with me,'' he gently reminded her.

''Yes. Thank you,'' she mumbled, blushing like a tongue-tied schoolgirl. Having a man outside her family care about her and her son's needs—a man as sexy and desirable as Alex King—simply hadn't happened to her since she'd become a widow. Up close like this, close and very personal, with the memory of their physical intimacy flooding through her mind, Gina found herself floundering in the situation instead of breezing through it with womanly confidence.

Alex simply took charge, ushering them to his big Land Cruiser, helping Marco into the hired seat and doing up the safety straps with practised ease, putting her bag in the back of the vehicle, then opening the passenger door for her. It was a big step up into the high cabin. Gina was trying to work out how to accomplish getting to her seat gracefully, acutely aware of Alex watching. He took the decision from her, scooping her off her feet and lifting her in.

''There! No problem,'' he said, the grin on his face tilting slightly as he looked into her eyes and saw she was remembering the passion that had triggered a similar action last night. "Couldn't resist," he murmured, and for an electrifying moment his gaze dropped to her mouth.

"Are you going to do up Mama's strap, too?" Marco asked.

Alex's swift intake of breath mirrored Gina's own breathless state. Her whole body was poised for a kiss, aching for it, but he pulled back and grabbed the safety belt, making much of stretching it across her and clicking it into its slot. "All strapped up now," he directed at Marco. "It's important to follow the rules."

He closed her door, and in the time it took for him to settle in the driver's seat, Gina managed to recover some semblance of composure, though inwardly she was buzzing with the excitement of knowing he was still as affected by her as she was by him.

"You didn't follow the rule of picking up your clothes," Marco stated critically. "Didn't your mama teach you that, Alex, like my mama did?"

Her heart stopped. There could be no mistake about what her son was referring to. No avoiding it, either. She felt Alex glance sharply at her and she rolled her eyes at him, expressively pleading for some innocent reply.

"Yes, my mother did lay down that rule, Marco, but I was so tired last night I forgot. I picked them up when I woke up this morning."

"So you were a good boy," Marco concluded with satisfaction.

"I was a bit late getting to it, but better late than never."

A strong hand reached across and squeezed Gina's. She squeezed back, grateful for his discreet and sensitive support. It forged a sense of togetherness again, as did the deliberate physical link. An exultant energy coursed up her arm and danced all the way to her heart.

"Okay?" he murmured.

She smiled at him, impulsively teasing. "You were very good."

Wicked pleasure leapt into his eyes. "So were you."

Three little words, delivered with feeling, and Gina's sexual awareness zoomed to a new high, coloured vividly by all she had experienced with Alex last night. She forgot about Marco sitting in the back seat, forgot to give directions to Crystal Cascades, even forgot they were going on a picnic.

Alex drove and she watched him drive, remembering how his hands had felt on her, the very male muscular strength of his thighs, the sheer perfection of his body, the sensations it had aroused in hers. She wanted to feel it all over again, and her mind sang with the certainty…so did he.

So did he!

CHAPTER ELEVEN

CONTROL....

Alex held on to the need for it with grim concentration as he drove Gina and Marco home from the picnic. It had been a good afternoon. He'd enjoyed being with both of them. He'd probably talked too much about his life, warmly encouraged by Gina, her interest even drawing him into reminiscences about his childhood, but at least talking had kept at bay the rampant desire to touch her, to recapture the incredibly intense sensuality that simmered in his memory.

Just the scent of her, right beside him in this cabin, was making it difficult to keep his focus on the road. Friendship was important, he told himself. It was more important than sex for any lasting relationship. But the very fact he'd felt she was in tune with everything he'd told her about himself this afternoon—understanding, appreciation, amusement so clearly in her eyes—made him want to leap into a deeper intimacy all the faster.

Not in front of the boy, he'd cautioned himself and that stricture still held true. Better to wait until Marco was more used to having him around, accepting him naturally as the man in his mother's life, the man who shared her bed. *And picked up his clothes!*

An ironic smile twitched at his lips. He'd give anything right now to be able to tear off Gina's clothes and his own, to have all the pleasure of being naked with her, making love. She wanted it, too. Her body signals had been positive towards him all afternoon. He was sure it was just a matter of reaching out, taking...

No!

It could wait. She'd invited him to dinner on Wednesday night. A return of hospitality for the picnic, she'd insisted. Marco would undoubtedly be put to bed at a reasonable time. He would have Gina to himself— a situation she must be thinking of, as well—the two of them alone together in a private place.

Anticipation spread a treacherous excitement. He tried to block his arousal by rushing into speech. "I'll bring a bottle of wine on Wednesday evening. My contribution to dinner."

"If you like. But you didn't let me contribute to the picnic, Alex."

"That was my penance and my pleasure." He shot her a smiling appeal. "All worries gone now?"

Her sigh expressed happy satisfaction. "I've had a lovely afternoon. Thank you."

The warmth in her voice left him in no doubt of it. As he brought the Land Cruiser to a halt in front of her home, he told himself to be content with having established a good rapport with her. And with her son, who had nodded off in his car seat. If Marco stayed asleep as Alex carried him inside...

No! Don't start something you'll want to finish!

The circumstances were still risky.

Just see them to the door and take your leave while the going is good.

With fierce control over almost-irresistible temptation, Alex went through with his plan, aided by Marco's waking up the moment he was lifted out of his seat. The little boy's bright chatter made cheerful goodbyes relatively easy, and Alex was congratulating himself on not having transgressed his own ruling as he walked back down the path to drive away.

A white sports convertible pulled up behind his Land Cruiser as he opened the front gate.

Peter Owen stepped out of it.

Alex paused, tension spiralling through him like a wire spring being compressed, wanting to be released with explosive action. He didn't want Peter Owen with his rotten smarmy ways anywhere near Gina. And what the hell was he doing here? Not content to screw Michelle, he had to try his luck with Gina, too?

"Hi! Been visiting my new partner?" came the casually confident greeting.

Alex unclenched his jaw. "Partner?" he grated out, barely containing the violent feelings this man stirred.

"Gina of the fabulous voice," he rolled out with relish. "Wasn't she marvellous last night? Your grandmother certainly made a great find with her."

"Yes, she did," Alex agreed, but not *a find* for the likes of Peter Owen.

"Thought I'd drop in and line up some gigs with her."

"On the off chance she was here?"

"Well, she is, isn't she?" He nodded to the veranda where Gina and Marco were still standing, waiting to see Alex go...or find out what Peter Owen's arrival meant. "Luck is running with me."

The claim riled Alex further. Owen had the habit of seizing opportunity and turning it into his playground. "Don't press it too far, Peter," he warned. "My grandmother wouldn't like having *her find* diverted. She's taken quite a shine to Gina Terlizzi."

Amused eyebrows were raised but the eyes beneath them were hard and cold. "Oh, the Kings don't own everything around here, Alex. People can make choices. It's up to Gina what offers she decides to take."

True, Alex privately conceded, and he'd have to trust Gina's judgement on this, but he hated the thought of this slime oiling his way into her life. He remembered she'd said a career singing on the club circuit did not attract her, and hoped Owen could not persuade her otherwise.

"Of course, the choice is hers," he agreed with a shrug, realising to play too protective a hand might well represent a stimulating challenge to a man who thrived on any stimulation to his ego. "Just make sure she knows what you're offering."

A cynical amusement accompanied his retort. "I never promise more than I deliver."

And that was short and sweet in Peter Owen's book. Alex hid his contempt, not wanting to reveal what he'd witnessed the night before. "Fair enough!" he granted. "Though I hope you keep her situation in mind. She's got it tough, being a young widow with a child."

"Well, maybe I can give her a bright spot or two."

Alex had to resist the savage urge to smash his face

in, wiping out the raffish charm he used so successfully on women. "I'll leave you to it then," he bit out.

Owen raised his hand in a mock salute. "See you around, Alex."

He had to leave. He had no right to block the path to Gina's door, nor forcibly turn Peter Owen away from it. As he moved to get into the driver's seat of the Land Cruiser, he glanced back to the veranda and was surprised to see no one there. Gina had obviously decided to take Marco inside the house, not waiting for his conversation with Peter Owen to end. Perhaps she thought Owen had simply been catching up to him and wasn't here for her. Whatever the reason for Gina's absenting herself from his departure, he still had to go.

It was up to her to decide on any further connection with Owen. It *was* her choice. Just as Michelle's little peccadillo last night had been a choice, too. People did what they wanted to. He'd find out on Wednesday night what Gina wanted. In the meantime, he had to curb his protective and possessive instincts and wait.

One thing was certain.

He was not going to be part of a triangle with a man he despised.

"Which video would you like? *Jungle Boy?*" It was Marco's favourite, and Gina hoped it would keep him occupied while she spoke to Peter Owen.

"Yes, *Jungle Boy,*" he agreed, settling himself on the lounge in ready anticipation.

Despite his nap in the Land Cruiser on the way home, he was still tired from all the excitement and activity of their picnic and it was highly probable he would doze off in the TV room while watching the video. Which would wreck his usual bedtime. Better that than giving Peter Owen fuel for gossip, Gina decided.

He was a gossipy kind of man. During their rehearsals last week, his conversations with her had been peppered with titillating bits about people he knew. Amusing but with a slight touch of malice in them. Gina didn't like the idea of being his newest bit of news, speculation running rife since he certainly knew of Alex's engagement to Michelle Banks. Being branded "the other woman" would be horrible.

It was disturbing enough that he'd turned up just as Alex was leaving. She had the strong impression Alex hadn't liked the coincidence, either. His back had gone quite rigid as Peter Owen had stepped out of the car and from what Gina had observed of their conversation, it hadn't relaxed him one bit.

It worried her what had been said. No doubt she'd find out soon enough. Her own urge to keep her relationship with Alex King private had driven her into the house, firstly to settle Marco out of the way, and secondly to put her bag out of Peter Owen's keen sight. His curiosity would be stirred enough at finding Alex here.

The doorbell rang just as the video came on. "Stay here, Marco," she firmly instructed. "Mama has to talk about singing with Peter Owen. It's business, okay?"

"Okay." His gaze was already glued to the screen.

Gina did her best to control her nervous apprehension as she went down the hall. This was nothing but a professional call, she told herself, though Peter Owen's decision to visit without telephoning first, didn't seem properly professional. In fact, she didn't like it at all. It was downright presumptuous of him to think he would be welcomed at any time. In fact, she didn't feel inclined to ask him into her home. It felt like an intrusion.

As a result, when she opened the door, she stepped straight out onto the veranda to do whatever talking was needed. "This is a surprise, Peter," she started off. "What brings you here?"

"The sweet smell of success," he answered rather grandly, accompanying the words with a smile full of charming appeal. "We were a hit last night, you know."

"I'm glad you think so, but…"

"Oh, I was lunching in the area and it occurred to me I should strike while the iron is hot, so I carried on here to lay out some ideas to you," he rolled out, explaining his presence and holding out the bait of future work with him.

Somehow the idea of being paired with Peter Owen—even professionally—made her feel uncomfortable. Last week she'd been focused on performing at the castle, in front of Alex King. Right now…maybe she was foolish to turn down a connection like this. Probably the more sensible course was to put the whole issue off until she could give it more consideration.

"I'm afraid this isn't a good time," she said apologetically. "Marco is tired and about to become fractious. I've settled him in front of the TV, though it may not hold his interest for long and…"

"Alex just brought you home from the castle?" Peter interjected, avid curiosity underlining every word.

"It's been a long day," she replied with a weary sigh, leaving the question unanswered.

"And you're feeling frayed," he chimed in understandingly.

She offered an ironic smile. "I am a bit. Was there anything urgent you had in mind, Peter?"

He reached out and ran a finger down her cheek as he pressed his interest. "Just don't forget how good we are together. I think we can capitalize on our duet act, Gina. Think about it. I'll call you during the week."

"All right," she agreed, though she didn't care for the over-familiar gesture.

His smile beamed approval. "Good girl!"

Inwardly she bridled, feeling she was being patronised, which of course she was, since he was the professional singer and much older than she was. All the same, *he* had come to her, not the other way around.

"I think I should tell you I only do weddings, Peter," she blurted out. "Performing in clubs is not for me."

"Ever tried it?" he bounced right back.

"No."

"You have a great voice, Gina Terlizzi. Time you let more people hear it." He slid out the understanding smile again. "I realise you're tired right now and your son takes up a lot of your day, but *you* have a life to live, too, and a gift that shouldn't be squandered." He raised his hand to ward off any further protest from her. "Sleep on it. I'll be in touch."

His argument carried the same attitude held by

Michelle Banks. Gina pondered this as she watched Peter return to his car. A gift…wasted. But was it really? She enjoyed singing, and she couldn't deny a good performance in front of an audience gave her a buzz. It was nice to be applauded, nice to give people pleasure.

Nevertheless, she had no delusions about how much work would have to go into pursuing and forging a career, and from all she'd read about the music business, there were far more lows than highs in it. Even with the step up Peter Owen might be able to give her, wouldn't he want favours in return for any success he brought her?

He drove off in his dashing white sports car—a status symbol proclaiming how successful he was? But how happy was he with his life? Two divorces behind him…

Gina shook her head as she went back inside her home and closed the door on an afternoon which had been more eventful than she could ever have imagined. She might have been more open to listening to Peter Owen, if not for Alex King's advent in her life. The chance of a relationship with him was more important to her than anything else and she didn't want to mess it up by not being available when he wanted to be with her.

Hardly a feminist viewpoint, she thought ironically, walking down the hall to the TV room. Marco had fallen asleep on the lounge. As she looked at her sleeping son, she saw Angelo in him so clearly, her heart turned over.

He deserved to have a father.

She wanted a husband.

Was Alex King the man who could give them the love and caring they'd lost?

Or was she chasing rainbows?

CHAPTER TWELVE

ALEX found Gina in the kitchen, mixing a dressing through a garden salad. ''Marco wants you to kiss him goodnight,'' he informed her, grinning over the fun he'd had, reading a bedtime story to the little boy.

Her face lit with an instantly engaging smile. ''I take it that Mr. Frumble has crashed everyone's boat in 'Busytown Regatta'?''

''With a vengeance.''

She laughed. ''Thank you for doing that, Alex. I must say, from what I heard, you put marvellous expression into it.''

He thought how marvellously expressive she was—eyes, mouth, voice, shoulders, hands. Even her hair swayed as she spoke or gestured. Poetry in motion, vibrant, evocative, intensely emotive.

And he found her clothes very, very sexy. A soft blue clingy top moulded the lush fullness of her breasts, its wide scooped neckline giving a tantalising accessibility. The long swinging skirt she wore wasn't quite transparent but through the blue and pink and green floral pattern he could see the shadows of her legs. It was a tiered skirt, ribbons and frills—very romantic, very feminine. Michelle wouldn't have been caught dead in it but on Gina it looked beautiful, flimsily frivolous, emphatically female.

She wiped her hands on a towel and gestured to the kitchen bench. "Everything's ready. You could open the wine while I kiss Marco goodnight."

"Will do."

He wanted to catch and kiss her as she swished past him, but contented himself with watching her, the natural sway of well-curved hips and a very provocatively rounded bottom, silver strappy sandals on bare feet. He imagined her wearing only a G-string underneath the skirt—definitely a blood-stirring thought!

A corkscrew lay next to the bottle of red wine he'd brought—a fine Cabernet Sauvignon which went well with most Italian cooking. It was, of course, an assumption that she would cook Italian, but the old heritage was strong, even though both he and Gina were born Australians.

He opened the bottle and took it into the dining room to fill the glasses she'd put out for them. He was struck by how much trouble she'd gone to; pretty tablemats, sparkling cutlery and china, scented candles, an artistic centrepiece of tropical leaves and little sprays of Singapore orchids, which reminded him that Gina worked part-time in a florist shop.

A pity she sang, as well.

The thought slid into his mind and Alex instantly pulled himself up on it. Her glorious voice was an integral part of Gina. She sang from her soul. To even wish to silence that would be a heinous crime against the person she was. He just didn't want her to be sucked in by guys like Peter Owen, used because of her talent.

All the same, a special talent such as hers should be

used. It would be wrong of him to get in the way of any chance she might want to take with it. But if she did choose to partner Peter Owen…

"Ready for dinner now?"

Gina swept in, carrying two salad bowls.

He was still holding the bottle of wine. Her sparkling warmth instantly evoked a smile. "Anything else I can help you with?" he asked, setting the bottle down on the table.

"The bread. I popped it into the oven to make it warm and crusty. It's a pull-apart loaf with cheese and herbs and bacon, but if you'd prefer plain…"

He shook his head. "Sounds great!"

Everything was great; the superb lasagne she'd cooked to her own special recipe with eggplant and mushrooms added to the usual mix, the tasty salads, the wine, but most of all her company. He loved the artless spontaneity of her responses to him, the entrancing lilt of her voice, the innate sensuality that flowed from her. It was a pleasure simply to watch her enjoy the food and wine. Not a word about watching her diet, not even when she served a deliciously rich chocolate mousse with coffee, happily relishing her own serving.

His gaze kept fastening on her mouth. Its softness and mobility fascinated him, its generous width when she smiled, the occasional lick of her tongue. He remembered its uninhibited passion, the incredible pleasure it gave moving over his body, its sensitivity, its instinctive eroticism.

Restraint was wearing very thin, the desire she aroused in him beating constantly at the gate of control he'd imposed upon himself. Surely she realised by now that this was a serious attraction, not just a physical lust he wanted satisfied. Though there was no denying the strength of the sexual element. It had seized his mind to such an extent he wasn't even aware he'd fallen silent. The anticipation that had sizzled all evening was surging into a burning need, searing away any other thought.

Her amber eyes seemed to have turned into warm liquid gold. Her mouth was slightly parted, but no words came from it, either. Her lips trembled. She scooped in a quick breath. Her eyelashes flickered as she jerked her gaze away from his to stare at the table.

''More coffee?'' she asked huskily.

As though sitting still had become unbearable, she rose from her chair, reaching for his cup.

''No!'' The word exploded from his throat. He was on his feet, halting her action, grasping her wrist, drawing her into facing him.

Her gaze lifted to his, questing, wanting the same answers he did. His heart drummed a fierce *yes* as he gathered her into his embrace and she lifted her hands to his shoulders, sliding them around to link behind his neck. He pressed her closer, his whole body exulting in the soft womanly feel of her, craving more.

Any last barrier of reserve was smashed by their first kiss. The fuse of passion was instantly lit and swiftly running, fuelled by taste and touch and the erotic scent of her, the real and intense ardour of her response. He needed the collision of flesh, needed her breasts bare, her legs open to him. His hands pulled the stretchy top from her skirt, scraped up the curve of her back, urgently seeking a bra clip.

She tore her mouth from his. "Not here, Alex," she panted.

"Gina…" It was groan of protest from every taut nerve-end in his body.

"I feel it, too." For a moment she laid a palm on his cheek, transmitting her own physical need as her eyes swam with the same yearning. "Come with me."

It was like a siren call, singing through his blood. Her hands glided down his chest, a lingering promise before she broke away from him, moving towards the door into the hall. Already she was lifting off the clingy top, her long hair being tossed carelessly as she drew it over her head. Her bare back gleamed enticingly, satin skin, broken by the white lines of a bra, being deftly unfastened.

Alex's feet were moving, following her bewitching lead. His hands tore at his shirt buttons. His fevered mind recalled Marco's chiding about dropped clothes. Gina was carrying hers, stepping out of her skirt as they headed down the hall. It floated around her thighs, her legs, and only a silky strip of nothing much left on her body, highlighting the soft curves of her naked bottom.

It was more erotic, more exciting than any striptease he'd ever seen. He unfastened his trousers, acutely aware of his erection straining against the frustrating fabric. He almost tripped, getting them off. She was trailing her skirt through the doorway of a dark room, soft lamplight switching on. Good…he wanted to see her, wanted every sense of her to be his.

She'd dropped her clothes on a chair and was facing him when he finally entered the room, her body lustrously silhouetted by the bedside lamp behind her. She looked like some wild pagan goddess, proud and primitive and breathtakingly beautiful. It made Alex stop to stand straight and tall himself, momentarily driven to match her naked dignity, to measure up as worthy of her choice.

It was a strange kind of respect but it felt right, like the squaring up of equals before meeting...and mating. He walked forward slowly, his gaze locked on hers, the desire charging through him gathering an extra vibrancy, a power that went beyond the ordinary. He dropped his clothes on top of hers, covering them as he wanted to cover her.

He rested his hands lightly at her waist, loving the feminine indentation above the flair of her hips. She ran hers up and over the muscles of his arms and shoulders, revelling in his male strength. He edged closer so that her large dark nipples brushed against his chest, closer, bringing her aureoles into contact, closer to savour the soft pressure of her lovely full breasts. He wondered if she could feel his heart pounding against them.

Her eyes seemed to glow with all the mysterious pleasure of being a woman, drawing him into her world, showing how it was to give this pleasure to a man. She swayed her lower body, rolling the hard length of his arousal across her stomach, moving closer herself to press her thighs against his. It was like having his whole body exquisitely electrified. Never had he been so acutely conscious of his own masculinity and the complementary nature of their separate sexualities.

This time he kissed her without all the pent-up need of waiting for days. He kissed her, wanting to explore every nuance of sensation she evoked, each seductive graduation of passion, of tantalising intimacy. Her mouth was like a treasure cave of rich, wondrous rewards every time he entered it. He moved her onto the bed, wanting to kiss every glorious part of her, feast himself on her femininity.

He wallowed in the lush feel and provocative taste of her magnificent breasts, grazed his mouth over her stomach, revelling in the erotic spasms of muscles responding to the trail of warm kisses and the sensual sweep of his tongue. He reached the apex of her thighs, felt the quiver of her legs as he moved in to savour and caress the most hidden parts of her sex. The moist heat of her was intoxicating, her responsive excitement addictive.

"Alex, please…" Fingers tugging at his hair, her body arching, yearning. "I need you now…now…"

Her words were like trumpets ringing in his ears as he surged up and over her, bringing himself to meet and answer her plea, elated by her need, and with the first exultant plunge deep inside her, the soar of his own pleasure was intense. They moved together in a rhythm that focused all his energy on feeling this sweet innermost part of her, the melting waves that clutched at him, squeezing, releasing. He concentrated on taking himself as far as this union would allow, revelling in the sheer ecstasy of pushing her to climax after climax, rolling through them, loving the throaty little cries, the erotic sounds of her pleasure, until finally, finally, he could not contain the driving rush of his own need, the fierce seizure of muscles that demanded release.

He heard himself cry out as he buried himself deeply inside her in the last ultimate act of mating, a climactic burst that spilled from him like tidal waves of explosive sensation, breaking into a warm haven that welcomed him and held him safe until he was entirely spent. Then the glorious contentment of simply lying with her, still intimately joined, embraced by the softness of her legs and arms wound around him, the lovely cushion of her breasts, the scented silkiness of her hair.

What more could a man ask?

She had given him—was still giving him—the most perfect pleasure he'd ever known…incomparable to anything else.

Words alien to his usual thinking slid into his mind— a state of bliss. He smiled over them…no exaggeration at all. Absolute truth. Then for a while, he didn't think at all. Basking in bliss with Gina Terlizzi was the best possible use of time.

It was she who stirred first, sighing, shifting her head so as to look at him, her face expressing a languorous satisfaction, her smile reminiscent of a thousand sensual delights, her eyes a darkly gleaming amber trapping sparkles of golden joy.

"You are amazing, Alex. Thank you for being so…so generous in your loving."

Generous?

He smiled, thinking how much he'd indulged his own

desires, yet it was Gina herself who had inspired them, the woman she was and how she made him feel.

"No, you are the amazing one," he murmured, lifting a hand to trace her lips with his fingertips. "You invite the freedom to give instincts full play and you let me follow them without any drawing back."

"Why would I? You gave me more pleasure than I could dream of."

"Then I'd say we're very well matched."

Her smile tilted ironically. "In bed."

"Oh, I wouldn't limit it to bed." He grinned teasingly. "If that lasagne was a fair sample of your cooking I'd be happy to share a meal with you anytime."

She grinned back. "I'm glad you enjoyed it."

"I enjoy everything about you."

Her head tilted as though she didn't quite believe him. "I'm not very sophisticated."

"Sophistication…" *if she was thinking of Michelle's superficial glamour* "…can be vastly over-rated. I love being with you, Gina. No false images."

She frowned over that last phrase and he wished he hadn't said it. A sour note. Yet in the next instant it led his mind straight to even more acid thoughts on Peter Owen and a pertinent remark tumbled out of his mouth.

"I hope you realise Peter Owen is a user, particularly where women are concerned. I wouldn't want to see you hurt by him."

Her frown deepened. "Do you mean personally or professionally?"

He grimaced at his urge to interfere, knowing it was seeded by a jealous possessiveness he didn't even like in himself. "I was just concerned when he called on you so casually last Sunday afternoon."

"I wasn't expecting him, Alex."

"Hey…you don't have to answer to me," he asserted. "I know he can be very charming."

"I meant…there is nothing personal," she went on earnestly. "He came about work. Some singing engagements."

He couldn't stop himself from asking, "Are you interested in taking on more engagements with him?"

"I don't know. I put him off. It was the wrong time to talk business. Marco was tired after the picnic. I'm to meet Peter tomorrow after I finish work." Her eyes held an anxious query. "I thought there was no harm in listening to what he has to say."

"No harm at all," he assured her, suppressing his own dislike at the whole idea. Peter Owen didn't have one moral bone in his body. On the other hand, if his professional interests were being served, maybe he would keep his hands off Gina, especially if she made it clear they weren't welcome.

"If he offers you a deal tomorrow, make sure it's a fair one to you, Gina. You could become a very strong drawcard for his act, so don't undersell yourself."

She gave a self-conscious little laugh. "Alex, he's the professional. Compared to him, I'm an amateur."

"You have a wonderful voice. I'd rather listen to you than him any day."

"Well, thank you, but…"

"No buts." He cupped her cheek and chin, fixing her gaze on his as he assured her of her true worth. "When you sang together last Saturday night, you were the star, Gina. It was your voice that enthralled the audience.''

"That could be prejudice speaking, Alex."

"Then ask my grandmother. She'll tell you. Don't make a quick decision with him. That's all I'm saying."

"I won't," she promised, though her eyes seemed to be searching his for other reasons not to make a connection with Peter Owen. "Do you think I should pursue a career with my singing?"

"Only you can make that choice, Gina. You know best what's in your heart."

She said nothing. Her eyes seemed to be wanting him to say more yet what more could he say? He'd been as fair as he could. He wasn't about to plead Peter Owen's case for him. In fact, what he wanted most was to wipe Owen right out of her mind.

He leaned over and kissed her. She welcomed him so fiercely, the desire to have her again charged through his entire body. Yet subtly, persuasively, Gina pressed her wish to make love to him this time, and Alex found himself so entranced by her kisses and caresses, he didn't want to take over.

It was quite awesome, the many ways she excited him; watching her, feeling her body move around his, the incredible sensitivities she aroused and played on. In some deeply possessive sense, it was as though she was imprinting herself on him—*her man*—and Alex couldn't help revelling in being so intensely desired.

Finally she straddled him, controlling the rhythm herself this time, voluptuously magnificent as she teased and took him to exquisite peaks of excitement, holding him there, holding him as though she never wanted to let him go. Her hair swayed over her breasts, a tantalisingly primitive picture, and it stirred the caveman in him. In a surge of wild energy, he swept her back onto the bed and took her, wanting to be the possessor, needing her to feel his imprint, and there was a savage joy in bringing them both to a triumphant climax.

She evoked so many feelings in him—more than he'd realised could be felt. Even as he lay with her afterwards, he was aware that the tenderness she drew from him was all-encompassing, an emotional level that no other woman had ever tapped. He didn't want to leave her, but time ticked on and common sense insisted it was a weeknight and they both had work to go to in the morning.

"Are you free on Saturday, Gina?" he asked, looking ahead to the weekend, wanting all the time he could get with her.

"Not really." Her sigh sounded rueful. "I'm booked to sing at a church wedding on Saturday afternoon, then later at the reception. I'll be taking Marco to my parents' home beforehand."

"What about Sunday?"

"It's free."

"Will you spend it with me?"

She hesitated. "Marco, too?"

He'd forgotten the little boy asleep just down the hallway in his own lovingly decorated little boy's room. As much as he wanted Gina to himself, he knew instinctively she was not the kind of mother who would let her son be ignored. Besides, he really liked Marco.

"Of course," he answered easily, his mind leaping ahead for some activity that would involve the boy. "I meant to check on the cane plantation. We can have lunch with the manager and his wife. They have a couple of young children. Marco might enjoy playing with them. How does that sound?"

She snuggled happily. "Sounds great!"

He smiled, thinking he'd take her on a long walk.

He'd never made love in a cane field.

There was a first time for everything.

CHAPTER THIRTEEN

"WHAT has made you so happy?" her aunt inquired, cocking her head assessingly as she watched Gina select precisely where to place a flamingo lily in the floral arrangement she was working on. "You sing, you hum, and your face is wreathed in smiles."

Gina grinned at her, brimming over with the wonderful pleasure of being desired by the man she desired. "Oh, I just feel life is looking up for me."

Her aunt arched an eyebrow. "Might it have something to do with Peter Owen?"

Gina sighed. "Has Mum been speculating with you?"

"Well, I know you're meeting with him this afternoon. And your brother, Danny, has just called to say he's on his way to pick up Marco."

"Danny's going to have a look at white-water rafting and he thought Marco would enjoy watching it, too," she quickly explained.

"Leaving you free…"

"It will be easier to talk business with Peter on my own. But that's all it is, *Zia*. Just talking."

"Ah…" She rolled her eyes expressively. "…who knows where it might lead. It's time you spread your wings, Gina."

Luckily, an incoming customer drew her aunt back

141

to the showroom at the front of the shop, cutting short the personal conversation. Gina was discomforted by the obvious gossip sessions running hot within the family circle. Of course, Isabella Valeri King's interest in her had set the tongues wagging, then singing the duets with Peter Owen at the castle had added to the brew of speculation. Neither had anything to do with how she felt today...after last night with Alex.

Should this new involvement be mentioned now?

She still shied from giving out such a highly personal piece of information. Even though Alex's invitation for Sunday assured her he really did enjoy her company— beyond the bedroom—she wasn't sure how deeply the attraction went for him. What if she simply had a novelty value, given his disenchantment with *false images?* Was that phrase a pertinent link to his break-up with Michelle Banks?

The urge to keep this part of her life private remained strong. One afternoon and two nights of being together could hardly be a called *a relationship,* not in any decisive terms. Maybe after Sunday...

Danny arrived in his usual rush and cheerful hustle. He was so accustomed now to working with tourists, his professional manner overflowed into everything. He collected Marco from the backyard of the shop and carried him off on his shoulder, both of them whooping excitedly about going on an adventure.

For the rest of the morning a steady stream of customers kept Gina and her aunt busy. Orders came in for deliveries to the maternity ward at Calvary Hospital— Gina always liked doing those happy arrangements, giving new mothers pleasure—and she was occupied in the backroom choosing the flowers for them when her aunt came to the door with a shock announcement.

"Alex King's fiancée wants you out front."

Gina was stunned speechless.

"Michelle Banks, the fashion designer," her aunt prompted.

"But…" She barely caught herself back from blurting out the engagement was broken. Yet if Michelle was claiming…or maybe her aunt was assuming…

"Apparently Miss Banks attended the wedding at the castle on Saturday night," her aunt went on, "and wants to discuss songs with you for her own wedding over lunch." Her smile was lit with delight at her niece's sudden rise to fame. "Your voice is now in demand, Gina. Better get going."

"But…" she spluttered again, totally flummoxed by these further statements. Michelle's wedding was supposed to be *off!*

"Don't worry about the maternity deliveries. They can wait until you get back." Her aunt actually rounded her up, thrust her shoulder-bag into her hand, and gave her a push, urging, "You can't miss out on singing at a King wedding."

Had Alex lied to her?

Her mind buzzing with heart-wrenching questions, Gina forced her legs to carry her towards a confrontation with the woman who shouldn't belong in Alex's life anymore, who shouldn't be calling herself his fiancée, nor planning a wedding with him.

Michelle Banks was idly glancing around the display

arrangements designed to catch the eye of passers-by and hopefully draw them into the florist shop. Her highly polished beauty instantly put another knife into Gina's heart. She wore a silk slacksuit in a shimmering grey-green pattern that picked up the striking colour of her eyes, and her golden hair was piled on top of her head, drawing immediate attention to her long, swanlike neck and the classic bone structure of her face.

She bestowed a lofty, slightly patronising smile on Gina, making her feel lowly, despite her average height, and definitely *common* in her little lime green shift. "There you are!" she said, as though she'd had to go to tedious lengths to find her. She waved her left hand in an eloquent gesture of frustration as she added, "You disappeared from the ballroom before I could speak to you on Saturday night."

The glittering diamond engagement ring on her third finger was as mesmerising to Gina as the swaying head of a cobra. And just as deadly to the hopes she'd been nursing. Alex had taken her out of the ballroom. Alex had kissed her, made passionate love to her, had told her...but his ring was still on Michelle Banks' hand.

"Your employer informs me you're free to come to lunch and I'd very much like to discuss my wedding plans with you," Michelle went on, exuding supreme confidence in Gina's falling in with her wishes. "Shall we go?" She headed towards the door. "I understand there's quite a pleasant little coffee shop just along the street."

Michelle opened the door, pausing to give Gina a look of arrogant expectation. It made Gina want to dig her heels in and flout the other woman's preset plans, but the painful need to clear up the situation drove her forward. She caught a glittery satisfaction in Michelle's eyes as she stepped past her to the sidewalk outside and gritted her teeth against the surge of sickening hatred it evoked.

Alex couldn't love this woman, she argued fiercely. *False images.*

Her frantic mind seized on the phrase he had spoken last night. Maybe he had let Michelle keep the ring when he'd broken the engagement. Maybe…yet why had she come, talking about her wedding to him? Who was lying? For what purpose?

Michelle prattled on about the duets with Peter Owen as they walked along to the coffee shop. Gina barely heard a word, too consumed by turbulent emotions to concentrate on listening. Michelle selected a table in a corner and quickly commanded the attention of a waitress. She didn't bother looking at a menu, ordering a Caesar salad and black coffee for herself.

Gina found herself automatically ordering a cappuccino and a Foccacio melt—ham, tomato and cheese. It was doubtful she'd be able to eat a bite of it but that was irrelevant. This meeting with Michelle Banks wasn't about having lunch. The order simply got the waitress out of the way. The moment she moved off, Michelle dropped her *social* mask and floored Gina with a sly sardonic punch.

"I take it you and Alex are still hot for each other."

Gina felt her jaw drop with shock.

Michelle sighed. "Good old lust. It does raise its

wicked head now and then. I hope you're not getting yourself into some serious twist about it. It only ever runs a brief course."

"You know? About Alex and me?" Gina choked out, reeling from this revelation.

Michelle laughed, her eyes dancing with cynical amusement. "Of course I know, darling. It was perfectly obvious on Saturday night that Alex couldn't keep his hands off you. I don't really fancy him making love to me while he's thinking of someone else so I told him to go and get it out of his system with you."

Gina's stomach cramped. They had discussed her as an object of desire before Alex had come home, come to the nursery suite and...she felt sick. The sex that night hadn't been unplanned. It had been premeditated. Her mind jolted through the train of logic Michelle was spelling out.

"But...you expect him to come back to you," she managed to say with a semblance of calm consideration.

"Naturally. We have a great partnership going." Michelle shrugged off the infidelity as though it were nothing. "A bit of bed-hopping makes no difference to the more solid things we share."

"And do you...bed-hop...too?"

Another shrug. "If someone tasty comes along. Actually, Alex was well aware I fancied someone else on Saturday night and was a bit peeved because he was frustrated over not feeling right about taking you. Had some attack of conscience because you're his grandmother's protégé. I told him you were a grown woman and if you wanted him, why not satisfy each other?"

"Get it out of the system..." Gina repeated, feeling she was dying inside.

"Exactly. We're just taking a bit of time out from each other at the moment, letting things swing."

"Why are you telling me this?"

Michelle gave her a pained look. "I just had the feeling I might have made a bad judgement call with you. A widow, wanting a bit on the side, seemed right, but Alex is a prize in any woman's book, and it occurred to me you might think you can get your hooks in and end up making trouble that could be embarrassing for everyone."

"So you want me to understand it's just a little fling that will burn itself out. Enjoy it while I can."

"Well, looking at it sensibly...what do you think? I don't mean to be offensive, but...Alex King and you?" Her eyes mocked any image of lasting togetherness. "Can you really see it, Gina?"

That was the crux of the whole issue.

And the diamond ring on Michelle's left hand kept winking its devastating reality at Gina.

Time out.

It made more sense than anything else.

No future with her...just time out for now.

Peter Owen sat in the Coral Reef Bar, sipping a whisky as he waited for Gina Terlizzi to join him. Normally it would amuse him to think of Alex King having it off with some woman other than Michelle. And serve Michelle right, the two-faced bitch. But Gina Terlizzi?

He shook his head. For all his cynicism about

women, Gina was different. Just a sweet kid really, open-hearted, devoted to her little boy, not the kind to play around with. Even he recognised that. What the hell was wrong with Alex King's vision? Blinded by lust? Peter frowned, never having considered the highly controlled Alex King that kind of guy.

Still, difficult to doubt Michelle's version of events since he himself had seen the man leaving Gina's house last Sunday. All uptight he'd been about Peter calling there, too. And no doubt about Michelle being totally peeved last night, coming to his apartment and spilling her anger out to him after finding Alex's car outside Gina's house.

"He's taking it too far," she'd stormed. "I'll spike his guns. I'll lay it out to her it's just a payback for my little dalliance with you, Peter."

"You keep my name out of it, Michelle," he'd retorted with very deliberate menace. Gina Terlizzi was serious business and he didn't want her turned off him by something that was utterly meaningless.

He took another sip of whisky, thinking he'd rip a few mats out from under Michelle's slippery feet if she screwed up the deal he wanted to make with Gina. He had plans for that girl. Not only might she give his career a new shot in the arm, but…if he took the job as director of musicals for the Galaxy Theatre in Brisbane and he could produce a new star…the birth of two new careers…

He caught sight of Gina entering the lounge and swivelled on his bar stool with a warm smile of welcome to put her at ease. She didn't smile back. She aimed herself at him and moved forward like a sleep-walker on automatic propulsion, no vivacity at all in her body, blank face, dull eyes.

Michelle had done a real number on her, Peter thought savagely, and for once in his life, felt a deep shame for even being loosely connected to this consequence. The slaughter of innocence was a miserable thing. He rose from his chair to meet her, to gently steer her to an armchair and see her safely seated.

"I'll get you a drink. What would you like, Gina?"

Her name focused her gaze on him, but in her eyes was a struggle to come up with an answer.

"A gin and tonic?" he offered, thinking she needed a good slug of alcohol.

A relieved nod and a huskily whispered, "Thank you."

Gina tried to pull herself together as she watched Peter Owen go to the bar for drinks. He might offer her some kind of positive step into a real future. Not dreams. Not fantasy. Something she could do for herself. It was important to listen.

Alex didn't like him.

But what did it matter what Alex thought now?

What she decided to do wouldn't intrude on his life. Not his real life. And however much she wanted to, she couldn't go to bed with him anymore, not knowing it was just a lustful fling on his part. That was too shaming, too humiliating.

Anger boiled up in her as she recalled Alex saying Peter was a user of women. How did he see himself?

Of course, he could undoubtedly defend his actions on the grounds it was *mutual* desire, and where was the hurt in that? None at all if she was like Michelle.

So what if Peter Owen was a *user!* Having learnt such a salutory lesson from this experience with Alex, she wouldn't be so stupid as to think there was any caring for her beyond the talent she had for singing. And even Alex had conceded Peter could be helpful in establishing a professional career with her voice.

If it didn't interfere too much with being a proper mother for Marco, she would try it. At least it would be something to focus her energy on, something that might lead somewhere good in the days, weeks, years that stretched so emptily ahead of her right now.

Don't undersell yourself, Alex had said.

How could someone who was worth nothing undersell herself?

Totally soul-sick, Gina watched Peter carrying their drinks back to the table. Whatever he offered her was better than nothing. Listen to him, she fiercely told herself. If Peter had a proposition that was workable within her circumstances, not neglecting Marco's needs, she would say *yes*.

As to what terms would be fair, how could she judge? She would have to trust Peter on that. The end result had to be more money for her anyway. So best to say yes. Go home with something positive to think about, something positive to look forward to.

The dream of Alex King wanting to share her life, be her husband and the father of her children, was gone, and she couldn't see any other man ever filling that role.

Time to start building a different dream.

"Here we are!"

Peter set the drinks on the table and settled himself in the chair opposite hers. No sexy flirtatiousness in his eyes today. He seemed to be viewing her with sympathetic concern. Was her inner distress so obvious?

"One thing I want to get straight first, Peter," she blurted out, realising there were some terms she had to enforce if she was to be comfortable working with him.

He nodded encouragingly.

"This is business, right?"

He nodded again.

"You have a…a sexy manner. I don't want you to come onto me in any shape or form. We sing together. That's it."

He heaved a sigh. A cynical disillusionment settled on his face. "If it's there, and I feel like it, I take it." His shrug dismissed that aspect of his life as non-consequential. "My experience is I'm no good at personal relationships, but a celibate life doesn't appeal, either." His eyes bored directly into hers. "I know it's not there with you, Gina. Nor do I want it to be there. It would interfere with business. So, believe me, no amount of randiness would make me risk losing your voice."

Could she believe him?

He leaned forward, forearms resting on the table, his hands spread in open appeal. "In this business, a sexy manner helps to sell a performance. It creates an intimacy with the audience. I'm not about to tone that down. On the other hand, should we come to an agreement, and I very much hope we can, at all times off-stage I shall treat you as my little sister. I don't want any friction between us. I want us to work in harmony to produce the best act we can. Okay?''

He looked sincerely intent on persuading her this was so. ''A little sister,'' she repeated, not quite seeing the very raffish Peter Owen in the role of big brother.

His mouth tilted ironically. ''I've never had a family. You'll have to teach me how I should behave.''

''No family?'' That was unimaginable to Gina.

He grinned. ''I'm just an orphan boy making my own way in the world.'' The grin winked out and a very focused energy was aimed at her as he added, ''I have learnt how to protect my interests and you come under that umbrella, Gina. You won't get any grief from me. In fact, I'll be the first to stand between you and anything that might have a negative effect on your performance.''

He was telling her that above everything else he was a professional. She could count on the success of their singing partnership being his prime consideration where she was concerned.

''Fair enough,'' she murmured gratefully. ''What do you have in mind?''

He explained.

She liked the plan.

It was easy to agree to it.

It felt good to have something to look forward to.

any friction between us. I want us to work in harmony
to produce the . . . . . .

CHAPTER FOURTEEN

DANNY was helping himself to leftover lasagne and
feeding Marco at the same time when Gina arrived
home from her meeting with Peter. The congenial understanding between uncle and nephew reminded her
that Marco had more than enough male relatives to take
the place of a father—her brothers, her own father,
Angelo's family. Her son was certainly not deprived of
male influence and interest.

"What did you think of the white-water rafting?" she
asked, managing a smile that projected interest.

"It was fun, Mama," Marco instantly piped up.

"Sure was," Danny agreed. "I think I'll get my finger in that tourist pie."

"Not too dangerous?"

"Not if it's properly run. They had a good operation
going on the Tully River." Danny, who was whip-lean
despite the mountains of food he consumed, pointed to
the lasagne left on his plate. "Better than Mum's."

"Different recipe."

He grinned. Even at twenty-four, he was still very
boyish, though very attractive with his sun-bleached
streaky hair and bright brown eyes which were dancing
at her with a teasing twinkle. "Did you cook it for Alex
King?"

Gina froze. Any connection now to Alex King was

153

anathema to her, and everything within her recoiled from having to answer questions about him.

"Oh, come on. Spill the beans," Danny coaxed. "Marco said he was here last night and read him a bedtime story."

"He called by," she returned stiffly. Impossible to deny his presence with Marco listening. "I'd left something at the castle," she added in explanation...*like Alex King in her bed there,* her mind mocked. "You know Marco grabs anyone he can to read him a story. Alex was kind enough to oblige."

"Alex now, is it?" Danny commented stirringly.

She grimaced at him. "Get off it, Danny. He's engaged to Michelle Banks."

He shrugged. "Not married to her, though. There's many a fall twixt the cup and the lip."

"Not likely in this direction. Now if you don't mind..."

"Okay, okay! So what happened with Peter Owen?"

"I'm doing a gig with him at the Coral Reef Lounge tomorrow night."

He whistled appreciatively. "Fast work! And classy venue!"

"Yes. Top of the line. Which means I have a lot to prepare tonight."

"I'm off!" He stood and ruffled Marco's curls in passing. "Be good for your mum, chum." He gave her a brotherly smooch. "Knock 'em dead tomorrow night. Got my own gig with the cane toad races so can't be there cheering you on, but I'll be thinking of you."

"Thanks, Danny. For today, too."

"No worries. Marco and I are buddies."

He left on that cheerful note, the Alex King visit brushed aside and dropped as inconsequential, much to Gina's relief. She needed to close the door on all her treacherous feelings for Alex and pretend the whole shameful affair had never happened.

Which was much easier decided than done.

Nevertheless, with determined purpose, Gina kept herself very busy for the next couple of hours, making sure her clothes and Marco's were ready for tomorrow, bathing her son and putting him to bed, making calls to her aunt and her mother, both of whom were atwitter at the news of Peter Owen's offer.

Her aunt insisted Marco stay with her tomorrow night since her mother was taking him on Saturday. Gina felt a stab of guilt at her very young son being shuttled around the family while she pursued her own course, but how could he come to any harm amongst people who loved him? She would always be the main constant.

Gina was still salving her conscience on that point when the telephone rang, no doubt an afterthought or extra piece of advice from her mother. Wearily she picked up the receiver, girding herself up to once more sound reasonably excited about her forthcoming debut on a stage that had nothing to do with eisteddod concerts or weddings. Never mind the dark misery dragging on her heart. She had a bright step ahead of her.

"Hi! What did you forget?" she rattled out.

"Gina…"

Her leaden heart came to a dead halt.

Alex King's voice!

She closed her eyes, trying to shut out a thousand haunting images of him.

"I've been thinking of you all day," he went on.

Likewise! her mind snapped. Though not on the same scale of pleasure as his tone told her his thoughts had been. Her heart revived and started catapulting around her chest, gaining painful strength as anger took over from shock.

"I don't want to wait until Sunday," he purred. "I was wondering if you were free tomorrow night."

Still hot for her and wanting a system overload before going back to Michelle! Gina gritted her teeth against the bile that rose at that thought.

"No, I'm not free, Alex," she bit out. "I have an *engagement*...singing with Peter Owen."

Proving there was life after him!

A pause, a sigh. "So you liked the deal he offered you."

"Well, let me put it this way. I know where I am with Peter. I didn't with you, Alex."

Her hard tone gave him more pause for thought. A tense puzzlement answered her. "What do you mean, Gina?"

"I had a visit from your fiancée today," she stated with pointed emphasis.

"I told you I'm no longer engaged to Michelle," he shot back.

"She was wearing your ring, Alex."

He cursed under his breath. "I let her keep it. Since

I was ending the relationship it seemed...ungentle-manly...to demand its return.''

Ungentlemanly?

A rocket of rage exploded in Gina's head.

''Was it gentlemanly to discuss your attack of lust for me with her? To plot a course of getting me out of your system with your fiancée's permission? Just a bit of time out to slake a temporary passion?''

''She said that to you?''

His voice rose in shock—shock at having his duplic-ity revealed, no doubt. Gina bored in, fury overflowing. ''Yes, she explained about her own *lustful* fancy for another man on Saturday night, and how such urges meant nothing in the big picture. A bit on the side for her...a bit on the side for you...''

''The bitch!'' he thundered, a mountain of outrage in his voice rolling over her.

It was just noise, Gina told herself. Nothing but dis-tracting noise.

''Actually, she wasn't bitchy at all,'' she said with commendable calm. ''It was really quite kind of her to let me know how matters really stood, stopping me from getting foolish ideas that might embarrass every-one. A pity you hadn't been more honest, Alex.''

''Honest! Michelle wouldn't know honesty if she tripped over it.''

''What a splendid marriage the two of you will have, bed-hopping wherever the fancy takes you...''

''You think I want that?''

''I don't know. I don't know anything about how you lead your life or what you want from it. If you were excusing what you did with me on the basis of mutual desire, let me state here and now I am no longer *hot* for you, and I am not *free* for you, not tomorrow night nor any other night."

"Gina, she was lying, manipulating…"

"For what purpose, Alex?" Ice dripping off her tongue.

"God knows!" Much heat from him. "Possibly malicious spite because I preferred you to her."

"For a novel bit of sex?"

"No! In every way!" he asserted even more heatedly.

"Like you can't wait to get in my bed again. That's why you're calling me, isn't it?" she bitterly accused.

He hesitated, possibly a bit of honesty catching up with him, Gina thought savagely.

"And you meant to keep calling until the passion burnt out," she mocked.

A swift intake of breath—quick, tense speech. "I appreciate—believe me—how clever and convincing Michelle can be when she's serving her own interests. For a long time she played a very appealing role for me, with only the occasional slip of the mask—a few discomforting moments that I overlooked because she dazzled on other fronts. But that's over, Gina. She might think she can draw me back to her if she gets rid of you, but she can't. She used the ring to cover her lies with a semblance of truth."

"A few hard truths, wouldn't you say, Alex?" she challenged, not prepared to shift from the ground she'd so painfully reached.

"Michelle's truths are not mine," he claimed with vehement force.

"Well, why don't you go and sort them out with her? I don't care for the role of meat in the middle, thank you very much."

"I'm sorry you were cast in that role, Gina, but it wasn't by me. And I will most certainly sort it out with Michelle," he stated grimly.

"I wish we'd never met. I've never been made to feel like…like a disposable person before."

"Don't say that. It's not true."

"The truth is…you came onto me too fast for me to believe anything else. A widow from the backblocks of Cairns…and Alex King—*the prize*. That's what Michelle called you and she's right. What else could a man in your position want from me except…"

"A woman with heart, Gina," he cut in. "Something Michelle never was."

"Then find someone who fits all your requirements if you're not happy with her. Goodbye, Alex."

"Wait!"

She'd already moved the telephone receiver away from her ear. Even so, his command came over the line loud and clear, making her hesitate for a moment. The instinctive tug towards him had a power that almost swamped common sense, but today's pain erected the barrier that had to be maintained. A brittle but determined sense of self-worth forced the receiver down—disconnection firm and absolute!

Before going to bed she took a sleeping tablet, telling herself she needed a good deep rest if she was to perform well tomorrow night. It didn't work as quickly as she hoped it would. For a long time she lay in the darkness, the memory of sharing this bed with Alex King last night too vivid to block out.

There was no denying she'd wanted him. He wasn't entirely to blame for what had happened between them. She had invited him here, madly bent on keeping him in her life despite the perspective Michelle had hammered home today.

False images...

The tormenting little phrase applied to so much.

The diamond engagement ring could be one of them. Michelle might very well have lied, aiming to get rid of any threat to achieving her own ambition. Gina wanted to believe Alex had at least been truthful on that score, though she felt he had come to her on some kind of swinging rebound, triggered by Michelle's desire to dally with someone else.

It could be the contrast that had drawn him—a woman with heart—but other things were just as important to the success of a relationship. Gina knew she wasn't his social equal. And as kind as he'd been to Marco, her son wasn't his. The Kings were like a dynasty. When it came to marriage, they would want their own children.

It had been utter madness to dream of something different.

She had to fill her mind with something else—the songs to be sung tomorrow night. The words were all about love...memories, hopes, yearnings, loss. Easy for her to feel them, she thought with bleak irony. Did a professional singer sell her soul? No, music was simply a way of expressing it.

The music of the night...

CHAPTER FIFTEEN

THE Coral Reef Lounge was packed, much to Peter Owen's satisfaction. Friday nights were always good business, but he'd plugged this evening's special performance on local radio this morning, organised the billboard to catch the interest of passers-by, and the response was even better than he'd hoped. The greatest songs from favourite musicals appealed to all ages—a sure drawcard—and he'd given Gina Terlizzi's voice a big wrap, as well. A star of the future.

He hoped Gina wasn't having an attack of nerves in the dressing-room. They'd rehearsed most of the afternoon and she'd been on fire, ready to sock the songs to the audience with all the voice power she had. Now all geared up in the bronze evening dress she'd worn for the wedding duets last week, she looked every bit a star.

The question was whether to tell her that the King family was here in force, Isabella herself with her three grandsons, notably Alex looking moody and magnificent.

Would it put Gina off or turn her on?

Once she was on stage and in the spotlight, she might not see them. The audience could remain a blur to her. It might be better to keep her focused on the songs— no distraction. On the other hand, the urge to *show* Alex King she could be a star in her own right might just

162

push her to that extra edge of performance that created magic.

Alex King checked his watch again. Time was crawling. Gina's debut on stage here was scheduled for nine o'clock and there were still six minutes to go. Peter Owen was doing his thing on the grand piano, warming up the audience, but Alex was incapable of appreciating the man's talent in these circumstances. His whole mind was bent on projecting to Gina that he was here for her.

Very publicly *here for her,* with his entire family in tow to witness where his heart lay, and it sure as hell wasn't with Michelle Banks. As far as he was concerned, Michelle had ceased to exist. He'd told her so in unequivocal terms last night. And threatened her with legal consequences if she used his ring to make false claims again. His fury over that deceit put an even finer edge on his taut nerves as he waited for Gina's appearance.

She had to realise he didn't view her as a bit on the side. Nor would he treat her as one. He'd introduce her to his brothers, make sure she understood that his grandmother was aware and approved of a relationship between them. Surely such a public statement would have its impact on the sleazy doubts Michelle had planted in her mind.

Isabella Valeri King sat very comfortably, listening to Peter Owen's virtuoso performance. He really was an excellent pianist. She was looking forward to the act he'd worked out with Gina Terlizzi. Though, of course, the highlight of the evening would come after the performance.

She was very aware of Alessandro's tension. And her other grandsons' curiosity. Their older brother's request for their support on such a personal matter was extraordinary. And the sheaf of red roses he'd brought with him had certainly raised their eyebrows.

Although both Antonio and Matteo had heard Gina Terlizzi sing last week, neither of them had known of any attachment formed between the wedding singer and their brother. The news of his broken engagement to Michelle Banks had come as a thunderclap, let alone this sudden piece of family stage management to impress a woman they hadn't even been introduced to. Tonight was certainly shaping up as of prime interest to all of them.

It gave Isabella intense satisfaction to know that Michelle Banks had completely obliterated any chance she might have had of retrieving a relationship with Alessandro. And her malicious meddling yesterday had vindicated Isabella's own meddling in this affair. It had also fired up so much feeling in Alessandro, Isabella could only hope now she'd done right in bringing Gina Terlizzi to his attention.

What if Gina was persuaded to pursue a career in singing?

Would she still be a good wife for Alessandro?

Marriage…children…it was still a worry, but not as big a worry as it had been with Michelle Banks. Tonight, Isabella was content to count that blessing, and hope for more.

*   *   *

Gina stood in the wings, waiting for her cue from Peter. She took deep breaths, needing to calm the tremulous state of her nerves. Her parents were out in the audience. Her older brother and his wife had come, too. The whole family was excited about this chance for her, and she was determined they should be proud of her singing tonight. No mistakes. No going blank on the lyrics or wavering off the note. Total focus on delivering the best she could give.

Applause followed Peter's last flourish on the piano. He stood and bowed, then strolled to the apron of the stage, carrying his microphone with him, ready to woo the audience with words which she had to live up to. With an ease Gina envied he jollied them into a buzz of anticipation, then held out his hand to her and with an encouraging smile, called her on-stage.

Her heart was pounding but she managed to reach his side without any mishap. Peter gave her waist a squeeze as they waited through another round of applause. "Isabella King is here with her three grandsons," he whispered in her ear, electrifying every nerve in Gina's body.

Alex…with his family?

"That's hefty support, Gina, so break a leg!" Peter urged.

The old theatrical expression for good luck barely penetrated the daze of shock. No way in the world could she have anticipated such a move from Alex—such a *public* move! What did it mean?

Or had Isabella King commanded her grandsons' presence here?

But why?

Why?

"One of the great musicals of recent times is *West Side Story*," Peter announced. "And what more fitting song to begin our program than Maria's and Tony's heart-lifting duet. Ladies and gentlemen, we give you... 'Tonight!'"

Heart-lifting.

No time to sort out the chaos in her own heart. Somehow she had to rise above it. Peter was moving back to the piano. He'd handed her the microphone she was to use. This was the kind of moment that separated amateurs from professionals. *The show must go on!* Never mind Alex and the King family. Her own family was out there, willing her to pull this off.

Pretend she was Maria in *West Side Story*—the modern remake of *Romeo and Juliet.*

Pretend Alex was Tony.

Pretend they'd just met and it was wonderful...a dream come true...before it was destroyed.

Peter played the introduction and Gina didn't have to pretend. She remembered how it had felt with Alex before it was destroyed and she poured all that feeling into her voice as she lifted it to sing, to soar to that ecstatic place where for a little time, everything had been perfect.

It worked.

She was fine.

Better than fine if the audience response was anything to measure by.

They moved on to the duet, "All I Ask of You" from

The Phantom of the Opera, then two of the most poignant songs from *Les Miserables*: "On My Own" and "A Little Fall of Rain." There was absolute silence throughout the lounge while these were sung, which was surely some kind of tribute to the touching lyrics and how they were interpreted. Even Gina thought her voice had never been so true and powerful in its delivery.

Maybe it was the spur of having Alex listening, or maybe it was the need to prove to herself that Peter's faith in her talent was justified. Whatever was driving her, she knew she was giving the performance of her life as they followed through the program Peter had plotted. Her last solo, "Love Changes Everything" from *Aspects of Love,* was an absolute show-stopper, much of the audience rising to their feet and even calling out "Bravo!"

Peter grinned at her, giving her an exultant thumbs-up signal as he waited for the acclaim to die down. Clearly his ego wasn't on the line here. He was delighted with the reception they were getting. He literally purred into the microphone as he acknowledged it.

"Thank you, ladies and gentlemen. To complete our very special program tonight, we take you back to *West Side Story,* to the song that encompasses what we most want from life. It's entitled "Somewhere"—that mythical place where even impossible dreams become possible. And so, I would like to invite you all to join Gina Terlizzi and myself in spirit on the magical journey that takes us… 'Somewhere.'"

It was amazing how quickly the audience quietened to listen, and their expectation was well and truly met when Peter started with no musical accompaniment, his voice crooning the words with such husky emotion, a lump rose in Gina's throat. She had to swallow hard before following his lines with hers, echoing the yearning and building on it. The piano came in, adding its spine-tingling notes. Then together, and in thrilling harmony, they drove the song to its soul-stirring climax.

For several moments after all sound ceased, the silence held, as though everyone in the lounge had been gripped by the song's heart-wrenching impact and didn't want to let it go. But it was over. The whole performance was over.

A single hand-clap started a storm of applause. Peter rose from his piano stool and joined Gina at centre stage. It was like being bathed in waves of pleasure. People called for encores but they had no more to give tonight.

"Let them remember the high and they'll come back," Peter murmured. "Just smile and nod."

"Is it always like this?" she whispered.

"No. You were superb. And it looks like Alex King thought so, too. Accept the gift gracefully, Gina. You're on show."

Gift?

She'd been trying to search out her parents from the crowd, deliberately evading any glance at the King group, not wanting to appear as though she was asking for anything from them. Her heart leapt skittishly at

Peter's prompt. Before she could begin to monitor her response, her gaze zeroed in on the man who should have no business approaching her unless…unless…had she hopelessly misread the situation between them?

He was in a formal black dinner suit, commandingly tall and stunningly handsome. As in the ballroom at the castle, people automatically moved aside for him, giving a clear passage to the stage. She could feel the power of his presence coming at her, squeezing her heart, raising flutters in her stomach, sending quivers of weakness down her legs.

Too frightened to let herself believe everything between them would ever be happily resolved, Gina couldn't bring herself to look directly into his eyes. She fastened her gaze on the sheaf of flowers he carried across his arm. The gift…it was the kind of tribute people gave to a singer at the end of a show, yet he must have thought of it beforehand, must have anticipated…what?

That her performance would be worthy of it?

Or had he intended to seize this opportunity to get close to her again anyway?

Glittering gold cellophane encased the flowers. A satin red and gold ribbon made a bouquet of them. As he mounted the steps at the side of the stage, she saw that he was bringing her roses—masses of red roses!

Her mind dizzied with feverish thoughts. The songs she and Peter had sung had been about love. Did Alex think red roses were appropriate for the occasion? Or could they possibly represent a more personal statement from him? *Love changes everything.* The words of that song were so true in so many ways…but she mustn't let herself get confused by wild hopes.

Somewhere a time and place for us… That was a hope, a dream. The impossible didn't really become possible. She had to accept the gift gracefully. That was all. Smile. Nod a thank-you. She was on show. No need to look directly at Alex. She didn't want him to see what her eyes might tell him.

"For you," Alex said in a deep velvet voice, presenting the roses to her.

She smiled and nodded. "They're lovely. Thank you," she murmured, keeping her gaze fixed on the perfect blooms. Dozens of them.

"May I invite you both to our table?" he went on smoothly. "My grandmother would like to congratulate you personally on a truly marvellous performance."

"For Isabella, anything," Peter declared. "I have always admired her judgement of quality and she certainly picked it in Gina. If you'll wait a moment while I deliver our exit line…"

"Of course."

"Thank you, ladies and gentleman, and goodnight. We hope to see you here again next Friday evening…for the encores," he added with that touch of wicked promise he did so well.

Laughter and more applause. Peter tucked Gina's free arm around his, gestured for Alex to lead the way and they followed him across the stage to the steps leading down to the lounge.

"Does my little sister want protection from the big

bad wolf?'' Peter murmured in her ear. ''I can run interference for you.''

She threw him a startled glance.

His mouth tilted ironically. ''Alex King is not here to give you accolades, darling girl.''

''What then?''

''To win you.'' He cocked an eyebrow. ''Are you winnable?''

''I don't know. It depends…''

''Shall I step aside and let him have his chance with her?'' he half-sung from *My Fair Lady*.

''Yes,'' she decided in a wild rush.

''Just remember you're quality. Real quality, Gina Terlizzi,'' he insisted on a sharply serious note. ''Don't undersell yourself.''

Amazing to hear Alex's warning about dealing with Peter Owen coming now from Peter's mouth and directed at Alex's interest in her. Clearly Peter had guessed something from having seen Alex leaving her house last Sunday.

She looked down at the extravagant sheaf of roses resting in the crook of her other arm. The cost of so many might not mean a lot to Alex King, but to Gina's all too impressionable mind, it meant he did not hold her cheap. But was he trying to buy her? Win another night in her bed?

She wanted him.

It might be a terrible weakness in her but…she lifted her gaze to the man leading them towards the table where he had his family gathered and she ached to touch him; to run her fingers through the hair at the nape of his neck, to curve her hands over the muscles of his broad shoulders, to lose herself in the strong masculinity he exuded from every pore of his magnificent body.

Was it only lust driving him?

Her instincts cried that it had to be more.

Surely the roses said it *was* more.

All she knew was…she had to find out.

CHAPTER SIXTEEN

SHE wouldn't look at him.

Alex pressed the introductions to his brothers. They responded admirably. His grandmother said all the right things. Gina had to know he was not intent on pursuing some hole-in-the-corner affair with her. She had to know. But she wouldn't look at him.

She laid his roses on the table. Her hands were trembling, revealing an inner agitation that he desperately wanted to soothe. She addressed his grandmother. "Will you please excuse me, Mrs. King? My family is here…"

She was going to walk away. His roses meant nothing. She wasn't going to keep them. Only courtesy to his grandmother had brought her this far.

He was seized by a wild primitive urge to grab her, hold her, preventing any escape from him, carry her off to someplace where they could be alone together, where he could…

"Your family?" his grandmother picked up. "I would very much like to meet them. Alessandro, please ask if they will join us."

"Of course," he plunged in, grateful for the lead. Control, he fiercely told himself. Meeting her family was good. Best it be accomplished right now, so Gina would be forced to acknowledge him, to introduce him to those closest to her. It forged a bond she couldn't ignore.

"Thank you," she replied to his grandmother, then hesitantly, "I'm not sure..."

Alex instantly appropriated her arm and tucked it around his. "Let's ask them," he said, forcefully denying her the chance of refusing on their behalf.

For a long, tense moment she stood absolutely motionless, staring at their linked arms, still not looking at him. Her face took on a set determination. He could feel her thinking, "Well, let's see how he deals with this!" Alex was equally determined to meet any challenge she put in his path and come out the winner.

For the next few minutes he focused on winning the regard of the Salvatori family; Gina's parents, Frank and Elena, her older brother, John, and wife, Tessa, all of whom seemed somewhat bemused by his personal interest in Gina and the invitation to join his family in a celebratory drink. To his intense relief they were happy to comply with the sense of *occasion,* pleased to be included in Isabella Valeri King's party, which meant Gina had no ready excuse to evade his company.

Nevertheless, he was acutely aware of the mental and emotional barriers that remained—silent but very powerful barriers of pride, humiliation, raw wounds that needed urgent attention.

He could count on his grandmother to play gracious hostess to the Salvatoris. He could count on his brothers to make them feel welcome. He could even count on Peter Owen to entertain them. A sense of civility forced him to wait through this last round of introductions, but waiting any longer was beyond him. Impossible to sit down and pretend a party mood in this situation.

Gina's arm was still tucked around his. He clamped his other hand over the connection to reinforce it, bent his head close to hers and poured all his willpower into a quiet command.

"Come with me!"

She didn't reply.

He didn't wait for a reply.

"Please excuse us. I'll bring Gina back soon," he announced to the rest of the party.

Immediate action, removing her from their midst, heading for the doors that led to the outside deck beyond the lounge. His heart beat an exultant tattoo as she came with him, not even a tug of resistance. Her fingers clenched under his grasp—a fighting impulse?—but her feet followed his.

The deck overlooked the channel to the marina downriver; rows of boats as far as the eye could see. The Terlizzi fishing boats were undoubtedly amongst them, boats his family had helped to finance. It reminded him that Gina was too conscious of such things, considering herself an *unsuitable* match for him, which was nonsense. Absolute nonsense!

Nevertheless, the fresh salty air and the imminent prospect of the fight ahead of him, blew away the heat that had driven him this far. To win this woman, it was reason he needed, not passion. Yet the dictates of his mind were lost in a surge of need as he drew her over to the deck railing and he swung her into his embrace, the desire to hold her to him overwhelming everything else.

"For God's sake! Look at me, Gina! I don't know what else to do to prove to you Michelle lied."

Finally, finally she dragged her gaze up to his, her golden amber eyes darker than he'd ever seen them, dark with an anguish that tore at his heart.

"Does it really matter, Alex?"

"Yes. It matters."

"Because you're still hot for me?" Her hands pressed against his chest, her body straining away from contact with his, her eyes sadly mocking the desire they had shared. "You had it right when you first kissed me. This isn't fair."

"I won't let you go, Gina."

"You will...eventually," she said with dull certainty. "I think Peter read it correctly. Your family...the roses...tonight is about winning. You don't count the cost. You just want to win."

"Owen!" A red haze of anger blurred any clear judgement. "He has his own barrow to push, just as Michelle did."

"At least it's a barrow I can fit into." Her mouth took on a wry twist. "Where do I fit in your world?"

"With me."

"The Sugar King? The chief executive of what amounts to a private bank? The heir to the castle?"

"I'm a man with the same needs as any other."

"More needs, Alex. You're no ordinary man. You may not have noticed when you barged in on my family, but they are in awe of you. How could they refuse a

King invitation? Your family represents a power they have never personally known. They don't understand this is about proving you didn't lie to me. You've pulled them willy-nilly into a situation that I'll have to explain, and what answers am I to give them?''

"I'd say the situation is self-explanatory. I'm aiming to have a serious relationship with their daughter, their sister, you, Gina!''

"An ordinary canefarmer's daughter.''

"You're not ordinary!''

"An ordinary fisherman's widow. With a child. Who isn't yours.''

"I'd be proud to have Marco as my boy. He's a wonderful child.''

"Yes he is! But he's not yours!'' Her eyes flared a poignant despair at his stubborn rejection of her protests. "What you want with me…it will never progress to you actually taking Marco on as your son, will it? You'll want your own children.''

Had Michelle fed her these lines?

Or had Peter Owen?

Michelle and Owen together, pursuing their own selfish interests, not caring what they destroyed as long as the destruction served their purpose. Thursday… Michelle doing her damage first, Owen following up with his proposition. Then tonight, feeding her the poison about winning…

Gina's hands suddenly curled into fists and beat at his chest. "We're not toys you can pick up and put down when you find something more attractive.''

"Neither am I!'' he retorted fiercely, dropping his

embrace to catch her clenched hands and contain the violence of feeling they emitted. ''Why don't you listen to me, Gina, instead of the people maligning me? Michelle wanted to get rid of you, Owen wants to use you. You're letting them screw us both over.''

Shock, agonised confusion.

''What of all you felt with me? Did that mean nothing?'' he pressed.

Pain in her eyes. A desperate searching. ''What did you feel with me, Alex?''

He took a quick deep breath, harnessing all his energy to answer her in convincing terms.

''Enter the villain,'' Peter Owen drawled, stepping out onto the deck and closing the door to the lounge behind him.

It startled them both into turning towards him, Gina tearing one hand free of his as she swung aside.

Owen gave her a crooked little smile as he strolled forward. ''I know I promised no interference, but it just occurred to me that Alex might colour me black, which doesn't suit me at all.''

''What do you mean?'' she shot at him.

He paused to light a cigarette.

Alex was sorely tempted to smash Owen's face in but Gina had left one hand in his and he was not about to release it. Holding her with him was more important than anything else.

Owen exhaled a stream of smoke, then cocked his head consideringly. ''Has he told you it was me in the garden with Michelle last Saturday night?''

A shocked ''No!''

Owen shrugged. "Well, he knows it anyway. And he probably thinks I was in on Michelle's plot to undermine your relationship with him so you'd see my offer as an alternative road to take."

"Oh, Peter!" Disappointment…pain…

Owen shook his head at her. "But that part isn't true. I may not have many morals, but I can see the difference between a woman like Michelle and a woman like you. I meant it when I said I'd treat you as my little sister and I'm telling you with absolute honesty, the mud Michelle slung at you was not mine."

"But you knew she was going to do it," she said flatly.

He nodded. "People do what they are bent on doing. I had no power to stop her. Michelle doesn't care for anyone but herself."

"Neither do you, Owen," Alex sliced in bitingly.

Another crooked smile. "Funny thing about that. I would have agreed with you last week. But I now find myself caring about Gina getting hurt. By you or anyone else. She has a great voice. It should be heard. I can do that for her. So don't use your opinion of me to rubbish what I can offer. That will hurt her, Alex. Her singing is an expression of all she is."

Alex hadn't expected that perception from Owen, nor the sincerity with which it was delivered. Had Gina touched something in his heart…tugged on his soul? It was certainly possible, Alex silently acknowledged, his contempt for the man shifting as a measure of respect weighed in.

With his usual air of flouting any criticism of his

behaviour, Owen took another drag on his cigarette, then flicked it into an ashtray left on the deck for smokers. His gaze held Gina's for a moment before moving a hard mocking challenge to Alex.

"The thing is…" he drawled. "My offer to Gina is genuine…and would be good for her. Can you say the same of yours?"

The caring was definitely there. Alex's mind was still adjusting to this incredible fact as the man raised his hand in a salute to Gina.

"Exit big brother," he said ironically. "I'll call you Monday. Okay?"

She nodded. "Thanks, Peter."

They watched him return to the lounge, the challenge he had thrown down—*will you be good for her?*—gathering a silent force that Alex knew was very much the enemy in tonight's battle with Gina. Yet in a roundabout way, Owen had given him the one weapon that might open her heart and mind to the truth that had brought him here.

Her singing is an expression of all she is.

Truth.

She had to recognise it.

"Those words you sang tonight…*love changes everything*…" Gently he pulled her around to face him. "You have to believe them to sing as you did," he pleaded with all the passion she stirred in him. "You have to believe love does change everything."

180   THE ARRANGED MARRIAGE

then flickered into an askance left on the deck for smokers. His gaze held Gina's for a moment before moving
a hard mo...

"The thing is..." he drawled. "My offer to Gina is
genuine...and would be good for her. Can you...

CHAPTER SEVENTEEN

LOVE?

Gina's mind struggled through the morass of thoughts
that had kept her in torment since...since Alex had presented her with the red roses.

Red roses for love?

The wild hope that had hit her then...Dear God,
could it be true? Please...?

With the helpless sense of surrendering her soul, she
lifted her gaze to the man whose love she yearned for
with all her heart.

A vivid blue blaze instantly seared away any doubts
about his holding anything she'd said against her. An
intense caring came at her like a tidal wave, crashing
through the apprehensions and uncertainties that had
been clinging on, fretting at a truth he was forcefully
laying bare to her.

"What are you saying, Alex?" she whispered, not
quite daring to believe.

"I'm saying I love you, Gina Terlizzi. And that definitely changes everything you've said against being
with me."

Her whole body tingled with the energy he poured at
her, carrying with it the determination to heal any
breach, to prove the way was clear for them, no barriers,
not even shadows of barriers.

181

Did it change…*everything?*

"I'm sorry I…I listened to Michelle," she choked out, shamed by the strength of his feeling for her.

"I'm sorry I ever became entangled with her in the first place. It was never right. Not *right*…" He lifted a hand to her face, stroking her cheek tenderly as he softly added, "…as it is with you, Gina."

She took a deep breath and asked, "How do you know it's right this time, Alex?"

No hesitation for thought. "I guess you could say I knew it in my bones the day we met. And the recognition just keeps getting stronger."

Instinct? Chemistry?

"I've never been hit like this before," he went on. "There have been other women I've found very attractive—obviously." An ironic edge there. "But what I feel with you goes much deeper. It's like you're in my blood, Gina, and you make it sing."

Yes, she thought, it *was* like music…big and overwhelming at times, soft and sweet, always emotional, passionate, tender, joyful, stormy and sad, as well.

"One thing I'm sure of…it's not going to burn itself out," he said very emphatically. "This isn't some brief candle. It's something essential—elemental—that goes right to the core of the man I am. Call it the fire of life. That's what you've lit in me, Gina. You are the woman it revolves around. And I'm not about to let it go out."

The fire of life… It seemed to Gina a perfect description of love—the magic spark that brought a man and woman together, making the heat that eventually gave birth to children, the source of heart-warmth that made life so much worth living. Yesterday, it was as though she'd been left with dead ashes, cold chilling ashes, and singing could never really take the place of the fire. All it did was reflect it in music. It could never match living it.

"I don't want it to go out either, Alex. I more or less plunged into a deal with Peter Owen because...because I was frightened of the emptiness...with you gone."

"I'm right here. I'll always be here for you."

Tears pricked her eyes. "I'm sorry I didn't believe. Michelle said things...things that struck true to me...like our lives were at odds with you being who you are and me being..."

"Perfect! You are everything I want, Gina. Everything! And don't ever let anyone tell you any different. Their vision might be messed up by things that are totally irrelevant to me, but my vision is very, very clear on what counts in my life. And you count one hundred percent. Have you got that?"

She nodded, the joy and the wonder of it momentarily robbing her of speech.

"As for the deal you've made with Peter Owen..."

"I don't know that I want to go far with it," she rushed out, not wanting anything between them spoiled. She heaved a long shaky sigh and laid out the dearest dream of her life. "The truth is...I mostly wanted to sing to my babies. Angelo and I had planned a big family."

Alex's hands slid around her waist, drawing her closer. "We'll have as big a family as you want. And I *will* have Marco as my son if you'll allow me to adopt him. I want to. I may not be the father Angelo would have been to him, but I'll do my best to fill that role, Gina. He makes me feel…" His smile held a whimsical appeal. "…I wish he was mine."

Her heart turned over. "You're…you're thinking of marriage?"

Burning certainty in his eyes. "I want you as my wife and the mother of my children. That's where we're going, Gina, if you're happy to come with me."

A fountain of happiness exploded inside her.

"But that doesn't mean I want you to give up professional singing," he went on seriously. "Your voice is such a powerful gift, I think the world should hear it. Owen's right about that. And I was wrong about him. I have no doubt now he'll do the best he can for you, Gina."

"I don't want it to interfere…"

"It won't. We'll fit around it."

His confidence, his absolute self-assurance about handling anything where she was concerned, held Gina in silent awe. Was it possible for every dream to come true? It seemed the brightest of bright futures was shimmering before her eyes and it was difficult to take it in, difficult to believe that the groundwork for it was being laid right now…with Alex. Alex King!

She felt such a huge swell of love for him, it lifted her onto tip-toe and her hands flew up to curl around his neck. "I was afraid," she confessed. "I thought you were bulldozing everything in your way, just to have your way. Even using my family…"

"I was glad to meet your family. I wanted them to know. Mine, as well."

"I love you, Alex King."

His eyes glowed with blue fire. "There *is* a place for us. I promise you we'll make it together, Gina."

"Yes," she breathed ecstatically.

And that place—*somewhere*—was suddenly here and now as they kissed, pouring out all the passion in their hearts, touching, holding, hugging the fire they'd lit in each other, determined on nurturing it through all the years of their lives.

CHAPTER EIGHTEEN

Dear Elizabeth,

I am pleased to announce that a wedding is now arranged between my eldest grandson, Alessandro, and Gina Terlizzi, a young woman who has my warmest approval. She is from a good Italian family, a widow with a child, who is the dearest little boy you could imagine. His name is Marco and Alessandro is soon to adopt him legally so I am almost a very delighted great-grandmother already.

You must be wondering how this has all come about since Alessandro was planning to marry that other woman when you were here with us. Following your very good advice, I proceeded to engineer a meeting between Gina and Alessandro, and a most fortuitous meeting it turned out to be.

As you so wisely said, nothing more could be controlled. Yet it is quite eerie, seeing them together, how right they are for each other. I am reminded so strongly of how it was with Edward and myself all those years ago. I feel very sure this will be a good and fruitful marriage, the kind of marriage I wished for Alessandro.

I hope you will be able to come to the wedding. I

enclose a formal invitation for you and Rafael. I will also be sending invitations to your three sons and their families. Perhaps their successful marriages will inspire my other grandsons, Antonio and Matteo, to think seriously of finding themselves a wife who will bring the gift of love into their lives.

It's been brought home to me that it really is a gift, and one that cannot be ordered or chosen. It simply happens when the right people come together. Nevertheless, in future, I shall certainly be on the lookout for any young women who could be right for my other grandsons. Having found Gina for Alessandro, I cannot be too far wrong in my judgement.

Thank you once again for your very good advice.

With sincere respect and affection,
Isabella Valeri King.

Modern Romance™
...seduction and
passion guaranteed

Tender Romance™
...love affairs that
last a lifetime

Sensual Romance™
...sassy, sexy and
seductive

Blaze.
...sultry days and
steamy nights

Medical Romance™
...medical drama on
the pulse

Historical Romance™
...rich, vivid and
passionate

27 new titles every month.

*With all kinds of Romance for
every kind of mood...*

MILLS & BOON®

MILLS & BOON®

Modern Romance™

THE BRIDAL BARGAIN by Emma Darcy

The Kings of Australia trilogy continues with a second grandson claiming his bride. This time a pretend engagement turns into the perfect marriage! As soon as Hannah meets her new boss, the dynamic Antonio King, she is thrown into turmoil by the fiery attraction that flares between them. And Tony is on hot coals, trying not to mix business with pleasure…

THE TYCOON'S VIRGIN by Penny Jordan

An enchanting tale of accidental seduction! When high-powered Leo Jefferson falls into bed after a string of meetings, he finds a surprise waiting for him: a gorgeous semi-clad siren! But the next morning his fantasy woman confesses to being the strait-laced local schoolteacher who fell asleep in the wrong room!

TO MARRY McCLOUD by Carole Mortimer

Look out for the second sexy hero in the Bachelor Cousins trilogy! Fergus McCloud couldn't remember how he'd first met Chloe Fox, but circumstances indicated that they'd slept together soon afterwards! Actually, they hadn't – but Chloe let Fergus believe it. Her mission was to prevent him publishing a book that would ruin her family – what better way than pretending to be his lover…?

MISTRESS OF LA RIOJA by Sharon Kendrick

An emotionally intense story with a hot-blooded Spanish hero… There had been a searing attraction between Sophie and Don Luis de la Camara, but she'd had to return to England. Now Luis had come to ask her to return to Spain – as his son's nanny – and *his* mistress!

On sale 5th July 2002

Available at most branches of WH Smith, Tesco, Martins, Borders, Eason, Sainsbury's and most good paperback bookshops.

0602/01a

FREE
2 BOOKS
AND A SURPRISE GIFT!

We would like to take this opportunity to thank you for reading this Mills & Boon® book by offering you the chance to take TWO more specially selected titles from the Modern Romance™ series absolutely FREE! We're also making this offer to introduce you to the benefits of the Reader Service™ —

★ FREE home delivery
★ FREE monthly Newsletter
★ FREE gifts and competitions
★ Exclusive Reader Service discount
★ Books available before they're in the shops

Accepting these FREE books and gift places you under no obligation to buy; you may cancel at any time, even after receiving your free shipment. Simply complete your details below and return the entire page to the address below. **You don't even need a stamp!**

YES! Please send me 2 free Modern Romance™ books and a surprise gift. I understand that unless you hear from me, I will receive 4 superb new titles every month for just £2.55 each, postage and packing free. I am under no obligation to purchase any books and may cancel my subscription at any time. The free books and gift will be mine to keep in any case.

P2ZEC

Ms/Mrs/Miss/Mr ....Initials ....
BLOCK CAPITALS PLEASE

Surname ....

Address ....

....

....Postcode ....

Send this whole page to:
UK: FREEPOST CN81, Croydon, CR9 3WZ
EIRE: PO Box 4546, Kilcock, County Kildare (stamp required)